VAMPIRE VALENTINE

LAUREN SMITH

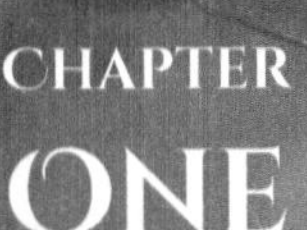

"You *know* I don't date mortals." Grace Stanhope glared at her friend Georgina, who stood in the doorway to Grace's apartment, waiting impatiently to be allowed inside. The dark-haired vampire grinned impishly at Grace and clapped her hands.

Georgina shoved her way into the apartment. "You'll want to date *this* one, trust me. He's adorable."

Grace rolled her eyes. "*Puppies* are adorable. A man should be . . . so much more." She wanted a real mate, someone who could handle her supernatural vampire strength. That meant mortals were out.

"*Please*, Grace. Just one date. What if he's *the one*?" Georgina gave a dramatic pause around the words "the one," as if expecting Grace to gasp in shock. Her younger self might have done that a century or so ago, when she had been human.

Instead, she felt old, worn out. She just wanted to find a true mate, someone who reminded her to live and embrace all of life's joys.

"You and Jake are lucky," Grace said. "Your potential true mate moved in next door to you."

"But he was mortal too," Georgina reminded her. "Please, Grace, just meet this one guy."

Grace headed into her bedroom and tossed clothes onto her bed with a weary sigh. She fixed Georgina with a look when she began to sift through the clothing on the bed as though planning Grace's date outfit.

"Why this one, Georgie?"

"Because he's special, I can feel it! He's the one for you. Just embrace the romance in the air. I always do."

Georgina flopped onto Grace's bed and lay in a swoon among the scattered outfits in a pose that once would have drawn in dozens of gentlemen to check on her and provide smelling salts, but men weren't so chivalrous these days. Thankfully, Georgina was no lady, not anymore, and didn't need rescuing. Neither did Grace. She'd gone a long time looking after herself. As a vampire, she had preternatural senses and strength. Despite her petite curvy figure, she was quite able to defend herself.

Still, it would be nice to meet a man who held the door open or stood when Grace rose to leave a room. She missed the small, courtly Victorian gestures that she'd grown up with, before she'd been turned into a vampire. It was silly to long for the past, but like most vampires, she tended to feel a bit nostalgic for the era she'd lived in before being turned.

"You know I'd never let you down, Grace." Georgina, whom everyone called Georgie, had been born a century before Grace and yet seemed to fit into the new modern world as if she was as young as any twenty-three-year-old girl on the street. Grace envied her best friend's easy, casual ability to move forward in time. Grace felt so stuck in the past sometimes, and modern life seemed determined to pull her farther and farther away from what she knew and felt comfortable with. Living in this modern age, she was torn between that old-world need to have a man desire her madly and wildly, and yet have her own space and freedom to live her life as she chose. It made dating, especially with mortals, virtually impossible for her.

"Spill it, Georgie. What have you gotten me into?" Grace tossed a herringbone wool skirt over her friend's face, and Georgina curled her fingers into the skirt's fabric, dragging it off her. "Or should I say, *who* are we talking about?"

"It's . . . Jake's little brother."

Grace's lips parted. "You set me up on a blind date with your mate's mortal *little* brother?"

They really needed to talk about boundaries.

"Yes, but hear me out," Georgina pleaded. "Jake's brother doesn't know about vampires—or anything that goes bump in the night or casts a spell, really. Jake's turning was an accident, and well . . . it's only been the two of them for so long. Jake can't watch his little brother grow old and die. You know what that's like for us. You lost William . . ."

Grace couldn't stop the wave of grief that followed. In that moment, she felt the weight of the many years that had passed since William's death. "That's a low blow," she warned her friend. "He died fighting the Germans. I lost him too soon. I never even had the chance to . . ."

She never had the chance to watch her mortal lover grow old and die. William had been her last fully mortal lover, at least the kind who had no connection to her powers from the supernatural realm. But he had been a true mate to her. She likely would never find another. A true mate was *everything* to a vampire. Mates were sacred. They were loved and cherished. Even the worst of her kind knew that a mate was something that should be respected. A mate was the other half of one's soul. William had been the sunlight in her dark world. Losing him had destroyed her.

"I'm sorry, Grace." Georgina resumed arranging outfits on Grace's bed. "But you have to meet Ryan."

"Why me? We have a lot of other vampires in our coven who haven't found a mate yet. Have you tried them?"

Georgie winced. "I have. We had Ryan come to a few coven parties at our apartment. He didn't know anyone was a vampire, of course. All of the single vampires gave him their usual inspections, but no luck on anyone being a mate."

"Why do you need to find him a mate so badly?" Grace asked quietly. "He's mortal—they don't suffer the melancholy we do when we go too long alone."

"Humans feel that loneliness just as deeply as we do," Georgie replied, her tone softening. "You've just forgotten that, but they do." She paused for a moment, her gaze briefly distant before she focused back on Grace. "If we can find Ryan a possible mate, he can be turned and Jake will stop moping about."

"I don't see Jake as the moping type," Grace argued. Georgina's mate was the definition of tall, dark, and handsome. Jake had a natural charm and build that any vampire would kill to sink her teeth into. And that natural appeal had only been heightened after he became a vampire.

"Well, he isn't moping. But he's worried, and I don't like him worried. If his brother gets too much older, well, it won't work. Jake doesn't want to have to explain to his brother when he's fifty why he still looks twenty-eight."

Georgina held up a black skirt and a red silk blouse, waving it to catch Grace's attention as a suggestion for what to wear.

Grace rolled her eyes. "I'm not going to go on a date dressed like Elvira, especially if he doesn't know about vampires."

"Does that mean you'll go?" Georgina swapped out the red top for a blue one, something they both knew would make Grace's eyes glow.

"Fine, but just one date. Then you can take him over to the Sleepy Holly Dating Agency if you're that desperate. They're good at finding mates. Glinda is a real wizard . . . or should I say *a real witch* at matching." Grace chuckled at her own silly joke of "Glinda the Good Witch," as she was called. She ran the country's best dating agency for supernatural creatures.

"You won't regret this. I promise." Georgie leaned in to look closely at her. "You know . . . you're looking a bit pale and red-eyed. Better drink up before you meet him.”

Grace cringed. If a vampire wasn't properly fed, their natural eye color gave way to the red glow that accompanied their hunger. She definitely couldn't go on a date with glowing red eyes.

“I'll get you a glass of blood.”

When Georgina returned to the bedroom, she handed Grace a glass of blood mixed in with Grace's favorite merlot. Grace drank it down and then fetched her knee-high black riding boots.

“So, let me guess, you have this little blind date all planned out already?” Grace said grimly.

“Well, yes. I mean, who wants to spend Valentine's Day alone?”

Grace hissed softly. “It's Valentine's Day?” She hadn't thought about what day it was. “No, hell no, Georgie. I'm not going on a blind date on Valentine's Day.”

There was nothing worse than an entire day devoted to thinking about all the loves of her past who were dead and gone. It was not her favorite holiday.

“Please,” Georgina begged. “You'll know after one date if he's a true mate or not. If he's not, you can have a nice dinner and a drink and go home alone. No big deal.”

Grace closed her eyes. She could say no, but she didn't want to be alone on Valentine's Day. It wasn't because she needed a man in her life, but rather because this was the one day of the entire year she felt the weight of her immortality and its terrible, lonely burden.

Maybe one date would be better than being here having an existential crisis.

"Fine," she half whispered.

Georgina squealed and zoomed around the room with vampiric speed, plowed into Grace, then hugged her as she jumped up and down and squealed for another minute.

"I'm going to call Ryan *right now* and tell him where to meet you and give him your phone number." She left Grace alone in the bedroom again, and Grace could hear her talking.

Grace took a minute to slip into the black skirt, blue blouse, and knee-high black boots before grabbing her coat. She didn't actually need a coat, of course, but she lived among humans and did her best to fit in around them. When it was cold, she wore coats. In the heat of summer, she wore shorts and shirts. She just avoided the sun. She could *technically* be in sunlight, but it made her nearly comatose, putting her into a deep sleep and requiring a lot more blood to snap out of it. So she kept to a nighttime schedule, and since her job was online, she didn't have to worry about any daytime job appearances.

"Georgie, come in and look at this outfit and make sure I look okay," she called out to her friend in the other room.

"So you're okay going into Boston tonight?" Georgina asked, holding one hand over the phone. Boston was only a quarter of an hour away from Cauldron Falls, where Grace and the rest of her vampire coven lived.

"That's fine," Grace sighed. She still couldn't believe she had agreed to this.

"He'll meet you at a restaurant called the Magic Pan in an hour and a half."

"The Magic Pan? How on earth did you get a reservation on Valentine's day? That's impossible."

"My suggestion." Georgina grinned. "It's owned by a chef who's a witch. She makes the most *magical* food. She's a friend of mine and I told her to reserve that table weeks ago for Jake and me, but I think it would be perfect for you and Ryan."

"I bet she does. If you tell her to add a love potion to my drink, there'll be hell to pay," Grace warned as she studied her appearance in the mirror and ran a brush through her hair again. Once upon a time, she'd been considered a perfect beauty. But that was back in the late eighteen hundreds. She had been a perfect Victorian woman, petite with curves, blonde hair and the darkest blue eyes that more than one man had composed sonnets about.

But times change, as do the standards of beauty. Now she looked average, and men were drawn by her vampire glamour. Glamour was a vampire's natural allure that mortals couldn't resist. It was the best way to lure prey.

She missed the old days of simply being desired as a woman, before she had been turned. She wanted a man to look at her like she was the only woman in the world and see the real her, not the being she'd become. Only a true mate could do that.

Georgina put her hands on Grace's shoulders and peered at her in the mirror's reflection. That was one thing Grace was glad was a myth. Vampires had reflections, at least in modern-day mirrors. The myth had come from the fact that old mirrors used to be made with silver as part of the layers of the mirror, and vampires couldn't see their reflection in pure silver. Modern mirrors, however, more often than not didn't have any silver in them, so a vampire could see him or herself just fine. If Grace hadn't been able to see her own reflection, it would have driven her mad. There was nothing worse than trying to style one's hair without being able to see it in a mirror.

"This is going to be fun, you'll see. Even if he isn't your mate, you can still have a nice time. Not all mortals drool over us, you know. Some don't even seem to be affected by our glamour these days. I blame the internet. Some of those social media apps I swear have spells layered into them to bewitch mortals into selling their souls." Georgie rolled her eyes. "Anyway, you can still talk and dance and do other fun things with Ryan, if you want, without it becoming a big deal. It's healthy to want to have a physical relationship with someone, even if they aren't a possible true mate."

Sex. Georgie was talking about sex.

Grace had to admit, she missed sex. She'd always liked it, despite being a Victorian woman when she'd been turned. She had a healthy appetite for passion, but she'd been without a romantic partner for nearly fifty years.

"I know," Grace agreed. "It's just that after Gabriel I feel nervous about the whole relationship thing."

Georgina sighed. "Gabriel was a warlock, a seriously jealous one, like most of them. You had one bad experience, that's all. It's time to let it go. It's been fifty years since you and Gabriel broke up and more than eighty years since William died."

Grace was 160 years old, quite young for a vampire. Some days she could feel the years dragging by, while on other days it felt like she blinked and twenty years had gone by in an instant. She stared at the mirror, but in her mind she was back in time, watching her warlock boyfriend, Gabriel, cast spell after spell to make her stay with him. Vampires weren't immune to magic, but the spells would wear off over time. Even the most powerful spells couldn't last on vampires.

She had fought Gabriel's enchantments time and again, leaving him, only to be spelled back into his bed. He had *used* her. He had never hurt her physically, but his spells had forced her to come back and say yes when she would have said no. That was a violation of her free will and autonomy, and she would never let a male of any species take that from her again.

As a vampire she was familiar with compulsion, but a vampire's glamour—their ability to lure prey to them —couldn't completely rob a human of their free will. It just removed their natural inhibitions and enabled a vampire to get what they needed: blood. Most vampires weren't sadistic and didn't go out of their way to hurt mortals. There were exceptions, of course, but most wanted to live in peace with humans. Gabriel had taken her will from her entirely and subverted her desires for his. She had been his puppet, his plaything.

Her stomach knotted at those dark, bitter memories. When she had finally gotten free of him and joined her current coven, she'd received support and protection from Georgina and the other vampires.

Gabriel wasn't able to touch her, not without risking a conflict with the London Blood Society. Even though she was now an American citizen and her British accent had long since faded, she was still part of the largest vampire community in England. Their protection extended to covens all over the world.

"Don't worry about Gabriel. He's in Los Angeles. Last I heard, he was dating that soap opera actress, the one with those fake boobs and no brain. I'm sure he's happy."

Grace drew her bottom lip between her teeth. She didn't want to worry about Gabriel, but it was hard not to. He was a part of her past, and at times like this his memory hovered over her like a dark cloud.

"You'd better go if you want to beat traffic," Georgina said. The pair left her apartment, and Georgina turned and called out to her as she walked toward her car.

"Have fun tonight, Grace. You'll love Ryan. He's just like Jake. Tall, dark, and handsome."

Grace chuckled and shook her head before she got in her own car. Maybe tonight would be fun after all.

THE SHADOWS CREATED BY THE TWILIGHT OUTSIDE GRACE'S apartment wavered and then began to shimmer as they took form. Gabriel Bonneville slid his hand into the pocket of his black wool coat and stared at the second-floor apartment where his former lover Grace lived.

"Oh Grace, my dear," he breathed. "I let you have your freedom, but neither of us has been truly happy, have we?" His little vampire was sad, lonely, and he could make it all go away with the right spell.

He entered the indoor hallway of the stairwell and went up to her door. He held a hand out over the knob. A green glow emanated from his palm, and the lock clicked open. Gabriel turned the doorknob and stepped into the apartment. He did not have a vampire's keen sense of smell, but he could see the energy that Grace had left behind as shimmering silver vapor trails, weaving patterns throughout the room.

Gabriel took his time in her home, picking up her photo albums and examining the desk where she worked. Grace was one of the few vampires who took well to change. Not all vampires did. Some seemed forever trapped in the era when they'd been turned.

Those vampires did not survive long in the grand scheme of things. But Grace, she lived almost like a mortal. She had bright colors and plants and things that reminded her of life.

Her bedroom was painted a soft lake blue, and pictures of bright rolling hills in Austria and landmarks from major European cities formed collages on the walls. Shimmering clouds of her energy danced in a silvery pattern on the left side of the bed where she preferred to sleep. That hadn't changed in the fifty years since she'd been his lover.

There was no hint of a man's energy here. She was alone. That should have comforted him, but when he'd tracked Grace here tonight, he'd heard most of the conversation between Grace and Georgina using an eavesdropping spell. She was on her way to a blind date right now with a damned human. Damn that interfering idiot Georgina. Gabriel had never liked her.

Grace's date wouldn't amount to anything. But if it did, well . . . Gabriel would make sure that Grace ended up alone again soon enough. Then he would appear, take her back, and all would be as it should.

Gabriel's lips curved into a smile as he stared at the silvery energy swirling around the bed.

"See you soon, lover."

TWO

"A blind date?" Ryan growled. "Seriously, Jake?" Ryan Harding stared at his brother, a frown twisting his lips. He wanted to throttle him for dropping the bombshell that he'd been set up with someone on Valentine's Day, of all days.

His brother grinned. Jake was two years older than Ryan and not scared of his younger brother in the least, even though they were both built like football quarterbacks.

Jake lifted his glass of wine to his lips and took a sip. "Ever since you and Mandy broke up, you've been lonely."

"I've been *busy*. That's different."

"Please," Jake argued. "You always made time for Mandy when you were together. Now you're just working yourself to the bone to fill the void in your life. Georgie and I never see you anymore. And when was the last time you shaved? You look like a caveman," Jake pointed out unhelpfully.

"I see you and Georgie all the time," Ryan muttered as he reached for the nearest reflective surface, which happened to be one of the pots hanging artfully above his kitchen island. Some designer had bought those pans and arranged this kitchen to look like a master chef lived here, but Ryan rarely cooked, thanks to his job's travel schedule.

He studied his face in the side of the pan, seeing two days' worth of stubble along his jaw. He didn't look like a caveman, but he did look like he'd been living out on some ranch and had just gotten back from a cattle drive. It wasn't far from the truth. He was a field geologist and traveled all over the country to oversee a variety of projects. So yeah, sometimes he looked a little rough, and he was still covered in dirt or dust, but who cared? He didn't.

"Anyway," his brother said, getting back to the point, "this is one of Georgie's best friends. She is a knockout and really sweet. I think you'll like her."

Ryan hung the pan back on the rack and braced his hands on the black granite surface of his kitchen island as he considered his brother's words.

Georgina, or Georgie, was Jake's fiancée. She was a beautiful brunette who sparkled with life and vitality. She was smart, funny, and easy to be around. Honestly, he couldn't be happier for his brother, current meddling in his life aside.

Ryan had met a few of Georgie's friends, and they were all nice enough, but he'd never felt an attraction to any of them. When he'd first met Mandy, he'd felt that mad spark of desire and attraction from the get-go. It was something both physical and emotional. He'd never felt that with any of the women Georgie had introduced him to.

"Have I met this one before?" he asked. "Was she at Georgie's Christmas party?"

"Grace? No, you haven't met her. She lives over in Cauldron Falls."

Ryan frowned. "That's the quirky little town obsessed with Halloween, right?"

"Yep," Jake replied.

Ryan had never been to Cauldron Falls, but every year the local papers in Massachusetts featured articles on it since it drew in a ton of tourism.

"She doesn't sleep in a coffin and wear all black, does she? I mean . . ." Ryan flushed a little.

"Grace isn't a goth," Jake chuckled. "She's *perfect* for

you, Ryan. I promise. Georgie has a sense about these things."

Ryan nearly rolled his eyes. "Georgie just likes to play matchmaker."

"True, but that doesn't mean she's wrong. Now go change. You have to look at least *somewhat* decent for your date."

"I'm still not sure I'm going—" Ryan halted as his cell rang. He pulled it from his back pocket and saw Georgie's name on the screen. "Swell."

Jake snorted a laugh into his wineglass. "You'd better answer it."

"Hey, Georgie," Ryan answered.

"So, has Jake told you about tonight? About Grace? She can meet you at the Magic Pan in an hour and a half."

The word *no* was on the tip of his tongue, but he heard someone's voice in the background. It was a soft, musical voice, and while he couldn't fully hear what was being said, something inside his chest stirred. Like a smooth stone had been tossed into the dark, quiet lake inside his heart. That voice made ripples on the surface.

Was that Grace?

"I . . . er, yes, I'll meet her in an hour and a half at

the Magic Pan," he confirmed. Ryan held his phone away from his ear as Georgie squealed.

"Bye, Georgie." He hung up on his brother's fiancée.

Ryan shot a dark look at his older brother. "Happy?"

The bastard smirked. "*Deliriously*," was his deadpan reply. "Now clean yourself up. Grace deserves a gentleman."

Ryan flipped his brother the middle finger and headed into the bathroom. He took a fast shower and shaved. Once he was done, he stepped into his closet to dig through the racks until he found a pair of charcoal-gray slacks and a black sweater, along with black boots. Then he grabbed his light-gray wool coat and headed for the door. His brother was waiting for him.

"You're leaving awfully early, don't you think?" Jake asked.

"I'm going to go grab a drink first." He'd looked up the Magic Pan on his phone before he'd gotten dressed and found it had a bar. He wanted a nice stiff drink to settle him before going through this blind date nonsense.

Jake said nothing as they both left his apartment.

"You off to see Georgie?" Ryan asked.

"Yeah. She's with Grace in Cauldron Falls right now. She'll meet me at her place later. We have dinner and dancing reservations."

"You crazy kids have fun," Ryan said with more affection. Even though Jake had pissed him off with this blind date thing, he still loved his brother. They were all each other had for so many years. Their parents had died when Jake was nineteen and Ryan seventeen. It'd been the Harding brothers against the world ever since.

"Ryan?" Jake called out as he reached his car.

"Yeah?" Ryan braced his elbows on the hood of his SUV.

"Keep an open mind, okay?"

"I will." He got into his car and headed for the Magic Pan.

He reached the restaurant with half an hour to spare. He told the hostess he was going to get a drink before claiming his table. The Magic Pan was packed, and soft music drifted through the air. The live entertainment in the corner of the main dining room played covers of famous love songs. Everything in the restaurant was in shades of cream and gold or soft blush pinks. It felt very romantic and expensive, which he didn't mind. His job paid well. Really well. He'd be picking up the tab, of course—his mother had raised him properly. Besides, other than his nice apartment and his new Bronco, he didn't have a chance or a reason to find ways to enjoy his money. So even if this blind date was an epic fail, he could at least enjoy the food.

There were plenty of others at the bar, but he found an open seat between two men. When the bartender glanced his way, Ryan gave him a nod. After a minute, the bartender took his drink order, a whisky neat. Ryan threw it back before letting out a sigh. Doubts began to creep in. What had possessed him to agree to this date?

I'm not that lonely, am I?

He tried to recall the last time he'd had sex, or even spent time with a woman outside of work. *Seven months.* Mandy had been more than a year ago, and he had rebounded with another geologist while on an oil job in Calgary. But that had been one night, and neither had expected more to come of it, so nothing had.

Ryan waited a few minutes, and the man on his right got up and left. A woman slid into the seat, and out of the corner of his eye, Ryan saw a waterfall of blonde hair as she bent her head to look down at her watch. Her hair was soft and golden, and he swore it seemed to have a glow to it. He looked away. He was here on a blind date, and he was not the kind of guy who was going to look at other women when he should be focused on the woman he was supposed to meet, even if they hadn't met yet.

"What can I get for you?" the bartender asked as he placed a napkin and a cocktail menu in front of her.

"A glass of rosé. Whatever vintage you recommend

is fine." The woman's voice was soft and smooth, and something rippled inside Ryan again. Was Jake right in thinking Ryan needed to get laid? It seemed women in general were somehow more alluring tonight than usual. Maybe he *was* lonely.

The woman thanked the bartender when he placed her wine in front of her, but she didn't touch it.

"Not a drinker?" Ryan asked the woman, surprised at his own desire to speak to a stranger. He was supposed to be focused on meeting Grace.

"What?" The woman turned to face him, and he caught the full force of her beauty like a punch to his gut. She wasn't just gorgeous. She was *exquisite*. It made him feel like he was a boy back in Colorado, hiking with his family through the aspens as their leaves turned that brilliant yellow-gold. A breeze had drifted through the trees, creating a flutter all around him.

It was a peaceful, natural experience, and it had filled him with a quiet sense of majesty and awe. This woman, this stranger, had brought back that old memory that had been buried so deep, he thought he'd forgotten it. She had drawn it out like the sun's light spreading over a darkened landscape as dawn seized the day.

It took him a moment to realize the woman was talking to him. He had been lost in her eyes, dreaming up a thousand names for their fathomless dark blue color.

"Sorry?" he said when he found control over his tongue again.

"I said I'm sorry too." The woman laughed. "God, I can't even *talk* to a man." She half muttered the last part to herself.

"You're talking to me." Ryan's head buzzed a little from the sound of her laughter.

"I guess I am, but what happens when I meet my date? What if I can't talk to *him*?" the woman asked, concern darkening her already deep blue eyes.

"I think you'll be fine," he assured her.

"God, I hope so. I hate dating, but that's the whole point of Valentine's Day, isn't it? My last boyfriend . . . Let's just say he was the *definition* of toxic. And it's been a while since I did the whole dating thing. It's all so different now."

"Your last boyfriend was toxic?" The woman nodded soberly, and Ryan waved the bartender over for another whiskey. "But you got away from him?"

She drew her glass of wine toward her. "I did." She took a sip, and then her face lit up with startled delight. "Wow, this is excellent." She took a larger sip and smiled. "I'd forgotten how good rosé is."

Ryan chuckled. "Been a while since you drank?"

"I have the occasional glass of merlot, but other than that . . . it's been ages." She grinned and took another sip. "So, are you here for a date too?"

"Yeah. Apparently, everyone in my life thinks I need a girlfriend. My last relationship, well, it wasn't toxic, but the breakup was hell. We were engaged, and I thought everything was good, then one day we both looked at each other and realized that the spark was gone and there was no love beneath it to sustain us. We'd been together for three years. Our lives, our property, even our money was so deeply entangled it took forever to separate everything, and that just made it all so much harder because we had to keep speaking to each other, keep seeing each other while we divided everything."

Ryan suddenly stopped talking and closed his eyes. He'd never said any of this out loud before to anyone, not even his brother. The weight of that truth, his failure with Mandy, had been such a burden on his shoulders. But he hadn't known how much it had been crushing him until just now. Once he'd said those words, it felt like he had shattered that invisible boulder. The weight of it was gone, and he could breathe again.

"Man, felt good saying that out loud," he admitted to her.

"Sometimes it's good to talk to a stranger. They can't judge you because they don't know you." She smiled, and the full expression hit him behind his knees.

"Yeah." He almost said that she didn't *feel* like a stranger, but that would have come off creepy as hell, or a cheap pickup line, or both. Still, it was true. Talking to her was easy, and he had this strange urge to share everything of himself with her.

"Oh crap, I've got to go." She bolted from her chair, grabbing her wine in one hand and her purse in the other. "It was nice to meet you!" She started to move away into the crowd.

He called after her, wanting to get her name, but after he'd tossed some money down to cover his bar tab, she was gone. He glanced at his own watch and cursed. He had to go too—his date would be here soon. He headed back to the reservation desk and told the hostess he was there for his table.

"Excellent, your party is already here."

"Oh?" Shit, he should have checked in first.

The hostess retrieved a menu, and he followed her through the maze of tables to a row of booths in the back. He skidded to a stop at the sight of the woman waiting for him.

The beautiful stranger from the bar stared at him in

stunned amazement. "Well . . . this is awkward. But I'll be honest, I'm not disappointed."

"I guess maybe we should have figured this out," Ryan replied with a grin. Suddenly they were both laughing, and the knot of tension surrounding their blind date vanished.

"So you're Jake's brother?" the petite blonde asked him.

"And that would make you Grace." He eased down into the booth sitting opposite her. "It's a good thing for us that we got the whole awkward meeting out of the way back at the bar."

"Thank God we did," she agreed.

"Well, I think it's safe to say we'll survive Valentine's Day without any more drama." Ryan winked at her. Inside, he was dancing like a football player who had just scored a touchdown. Tonight was going to be fun, he just knew it.

He was gorgeous. That was the first thing Grace noticed about Ryan, even though it made her feel shallow. Yes, her fatal flaw was falling hard for someone's looks before she even got to know them. And those penetrating eyes, hard sculpted jawline, and muscular body had hit all the right buttons. She was a vampire, but she was still a woman.

He was ruggedly handsome in a wonderfully wild way, and a vitality emanated from him that reminded her of herself when she'd still been human. Even though she'd grown up in an oppressive Victorian society, she'd had a rare slice of freedom thanks to a doting father and a progressive mother. She'd been allowed to ride through the fields on horseback and sprint about on the roads by her home with her skirts held up above her knees.

Those early years, with sunlight on her face, the wind whipping through her skirts and her hair tangling as she frolicked in the joy of being alive . . . God, she missed that. Missed the sensation of breath pushing in and out of her lungs, of feeling like a part of something bigger in the universe. Just looking at Ryan, hearing his voice, it made her feel like she was alive again.

Georgie was right. He was tall, dark, and gorgeous, even more so than his brother, Jake, if that was possible. Still, there was something more to Ryan Harding than just his looks.

"So, Grace, what do you do for a living?" Ryan asked. "I figured we should get those pesky standard questions out of the way first, don't you? Maybe Jake and Georgie should have had us fill out questionnaires before we left?" His lips twitched in a hint of a smile. He was teasing her, and she found she liked it immensely.

"I work in the online marketing department of a children's book publisher."

"Really?" He leaned forward. "What do you do for them?"

"It's a mixture of creating and running ad campaigns on major retail sites that sell the books. We create graphics and run analyses on cost-per-click bids for each campaign."

"I had no idea so much marketing goes into that."

"Oh yeah, it's a ton of work, but it's work I love. Children's literature is a place of magic. Every story a child reads enriches their mental growth, their imagination. The children who read are the children who dream. The world is losing true dreamers. I see children these days who play games on digital tablets but can't even read. Those children lose so much time developing their communication and critical thinking skills. It breaks my heart, really. Children's books are so important for our culture's survival and growth." She halted when she realized she was babbling. "Wow, sorry. I don't normally just—"

Ryan reached across the table and grasped her

hand. A pulse shot up her arm from the place his warm, strong fingers curled around hers.

"Never apologize for something you're passionate about. It's important to love what you do and to see the need for it."

"I agree. I'm just not usually so talkative." When she'd been with Gabriel, she'd always had to agree with him on whatever he said. Had to listen to him and his opinions. She'd always come second, an accessory to the life he felt he deserved. But here she was with Ryan, talking, opening up, and just enjoying being herself.

"So what about you?" she asked.

Ryan's rich dark eyes were soft and yet full of intensity.

"I'm a geologist. Now, before you run or fall asleep, let me assure you it's not just about looking at rocks . . ." Ryan hesitated. "I'm not boring you already, am I?"

"Nope," she promised and sipped her wine. It tasted *divine,* more divine than it had an hour ago when she'd drunk that merlot with blood that Georgie had given her. As a vampire, she'd lost her appetite for food a long time ago and lived mainly on blood, which was all that was necessary, but right then, her wine tasted simply amazing...Had the witch who owned this place put love spells in the drinks?

"So, rocks . . ." Ryan cleared his throat as if he was a

little embarrassed, but still delighted to be talking. "The amazing thing about them is that they are ancient, the oldest surviving parts of our planet. When I'm examining beds of rock that have pushed up to the surface after some seismic shift, I'm connecting myself back billions of years. Stones hold memories.

"I've placed my hand inside the tracks left behind by dinosaurs. They've become a tangible memory of the creatures who came before. It's humbling. A lot of people feel small when they really understand how old the earth is. How little time they've been on it. But not me. Every atom in my body, it was here in some form or another right from the beginning, as dirt, plant, animal . . . even stardust. The atoms that live within me have come to life a million times over, and when I die, they will live again somewhere else. Perhaps I'll be part of a thousand sea creatures or part of the bedrock of a mountain. Whatever happens, I'll still be here, a part of life." Ryan's face turned ruddy. "God, I must sound like a lunatic." He eyed his glass of whiskey suspiciously. "No more drinks for me tonight, I think." He pushed away his empty glass.

For a long second, Grace held on to his words. As a vampire, she was unchanged. She was removed from life's natural cycle. She'd known that, but she'd never really faced the sorrow that knowledge created. She'd always felt like she was on the outside looking in on a beautiful world within a snowglobe that was no longer meant to be hers, the land of the living, breathing, and dying creatures. As a vampire, she was neither dead nor alive; she was simply *undead*, existing in a realm that defied nature. Yet, the way he'd spoken about life, she realized that one day she would die, in whatever way vampires did, and she too would become part of the earth again, part of some new life. She wasn't trapped, not like she'd always thought she was. He'd given her hope that someday she would change and follow the path of other living creatures. He would never know the gift he'd just given her.

"I'm sorry," he said quietly. "I knew that was a mistake. Most people don't want to—"

"No, I like hearing you talk. You're honest and real. I just wasn't expecting that." They were still holding hands, and she realized she was stroking a thumb against his wrist, her mind tracking his steady pulse.

"Keep talking," she encouraged him. "I like listening to you."

He smiled bashfully. The boyish expression on such a masculine face was surprisingly charming. For a second she imagined him smiling at her like that before she kissed his neck and sank her teeth into him.

The ache in her fangs reminded her that she needed

to feed again soon. She had brought some blood in her car like she always did for emergencies, but she couldn't get to it until after dinner.

He went on to explain how he visited oil field sites and new building locations, and how he examined and assessed them.

"So you travel a lot."

"I do. I used to like it, but now I'm thinking it might be nice to stay in one place for a while." He paused, and his gaze turned pensive. "Or perhaps meet someone who wouldn't mind traveling with me."

Grace opened her mouth to ask him more about what he was looking for in a romantic partner, but suddenly the fine hairs stood up on the back of her neck. She had honed instincts to sense prey, but she could also detect other predators when they came close. There was only one person who ever sent tingles down her spine that way, and it wasn't someone she wanted to meet ever again. Yet there he was.

Gabriel strolled down the row of dining tables toward them. His pale blue eyes held the glitter of dark magic. He was addicted to it, the way some people were addicted to drugs. The more of it he used, the darker his heart became. She knew Gabriel didn't want to hurt her, but he wanted to use her, possess her, and she'd sworn she'd never let that happen again.

How had he found her? What was he doing here? He was supposed to be in Los Angeles shacked up with some soap opera star. They hadn't seen each other for half a century.

"Grace. How lovely to see you." Gabriel deliberately didn't look at Ryan. Ryan leaned back in his chair. He seemed to study Gabriel curiously. Most mortal men would back away or avert their gaze. It was a natural reaction to Gabriel's power, even though mortals didn't know *why* they felt compelled to steer clear of him. But Ryan showed no signs of cowering.

"How long has it been since we've seen each other?" Gabriel asked.

"Not long enough," Grace replied icily.

"I miss you." Gabriel's voice oozed charm and romance, but she could hear the ringing falseness behind his bewitching words.

"The feeling is not mutual," she said simply and stared into his eyes, eyes that held only pain for her. "There is nothing to resurrect between us, Gabriel. Please leave."

Only then did Gabriel's gaze flick to Ryan and back to her. Gabriel chuckled softly.

"It's dangerous out there, dating in the *super* world." He said the word *super* with extra emphasis.

Thankfully, Ryan didn't have any idea what Gabriel was referring to.

"Grace, would you like me to escort this man to the door? Or perhaps the nearest trash can?" Ryan's voice was low, the threat clear.

Gabriel responded with a lazy grin that would've made Grace's blood boil if she had still been human. "You couldn't make me if you tried."

"You might be surprised." Ryan didn't move, but Grace now realized that while he may be human, he was not prey. Not even close. That realization made her body hum with appreciation. Ryan was mortal, but he wasn't weak.

"That won't be necessary. Gabriel was just leaving, weren't you?" Grace let out a faint hiss that only the warlock would hear. She would fight him if need be, public setting be damned. Gabriel wisely took her warning seriously and left the restaurant, but he took his time strolling toward the door.

"Let me guess, that was your toxic ex-boyfriend?"

"Unfortunately."

"Well, we got the worst part of the evening out of the way, then. We can check *toxic ex-boyfriend meetups* off the list." He raised his water glass in a toast, and she did the same. The tension Gabriel's unexpected arrival had stirred faded away. The food arrived and the aromas wafting off the plates made Grace's mouth water. She couldn't remember the last time she'd been hungry for human food. But then, the chef who ran the restaurant was a witch who was no stranger to serving her kind and used enchantments to enhance the flavors.

Grace lifted her fork for a bite of her shrimp scampi and froze in realization. *Her appetite for mortal food was back.*

The main cause of human appetites reemerging was when a vampire was in the presence of a true mate. Her gaze locked on Ryan, stunned.

Was it possible? For the first time in a long while, she was unsure what to do. The idea that he might be her mate made her feel both free and shy at the same time, and the conflicting emotions left her on edge.

But Ryan made conversation easy, and the food was divine. Soon her uncertainty was fading. Maybe Georgie was right. This blind date thing wasn't so bad, and the man across from her staring at her with a ravenous look that matched her own might be her true mate. Perhaps Valentine's Day didn't suck after all.

THREE

Gabriel scowled as he stared at the clear vial in his hand. He raised it up in the moonlight and examined the three golden strands of Grace's hair he'd placed within it. He'd retrieved the strands when he'd been in her apartment.

He hadn't wanted to resort to spellcraft, but now it seemed he would have to. It was the only way to keep her away from that *human*. Grace would never walk away from a possible true mate.

It had been so clear, even to Gabriel. The silvery energy around Grace matched the golden light that swirled around the mortal man sitting with her. It was something he had only seen between true mates or possible true mates in the supernatural world.

A better man would have left Grace and her new

mate alone, but Gabriel had never professed to be a good man. He had learned early on in life that with his power he had the chance to take what he wanted, and if he didn't, someone else would. Such was the way of the world. If he wanted Grace, then he would have her, true mate be damned.

He tucked the vial into his coat pocket and got into his car. He traveled to a rough part of Boston where he had plenty of contacts for acquiring black-market items for his spells. He wasn't spellcasting tonight, however.

The seedy bar he entered was dimly lit and full of tobacco smoke, allowing the denizens inside to cloak themselves in shadows. Gabriel headed for the bar and removed a double-sided coin from his pocket. It was bewitched so as to make anyone who looked upon it not think too hard about their decisions.

He caught the bartender's attention and twirled the coin between his fingers as if performing an absent-minded magician's trick. But this was no parlor trick. Real magic pulsed through him into the coin, and a glimmer of light flickered against the bartender's face as he stared at it rather than Gabriel.

"What can I get you?" the bartender asked, his gaze slightly unfocused.

"Information," Gabriel said.

"What kind?" the bartender replied.

Gabriel smiled. "The kind where you point me in the direction of a killer."

The bartender blinked and finally met Gabriel's eyes. "What is it you're wanting to slay?

"A vampire slayer will do." He slid a wad of cash across the bar toward the man.

"The corner table in the back. He'll be what you're looking for." The bartender gave a nod in the direction he meant for Gabriel to look, and Gabriel slowly turned around.

"Thanks." Gabriel meandered through the smoky bar toward that distant table where a man sat nursing a glass of bourbon. He sat down and removed a photograph of Grace and slid it across the bar toward the man.

"I was told you could help me with a problem. The kind that requires a pointy little wooden stake."

The man was in his early forties, and he wore black pants and a black military-issue sweater. His face was carved with lines, despite the fact that he didn't seem old enough to be so marked. He'd lived a rough life. Hunting supernatural creatures was a dangerous business. The man frowned as he took the picture of Grace and examined it.

"You got an undead problem?"

"Yes, I do. This woman and her male vampire mate

have been feeding on people. They've killed dozens of innocent people in the last month. I can tell you where to find them."

"It'll be five thousand for them both," the man warned and finished his bourbon. "It's more dangerous to take on a mated pair. They tend to take it personal when one of them dies."

"Money is not a problem." Gabriel placed a wad of hundreds on the table, and the man snatch them up.

"Tell me everything about your vampires."

Gabriel smiled. Grace would survive an encounter with this fool, but if Gabriel was lucky, the man would kill Grace's human mate first.

RYAN NOTICED THEIR SERVER EYEING HIM AND DELIBERATELY checking his watch. Ryan glanced at his own wrist and flinched. It was nearly eleven. He and Grace had been talking for three hours. The restaurant was completely empty around them.

"Oh my," Grace murmured. "I think they closed thirty minutes ago."

"I'll leave them a big tip." Ryan left two hundred dollars on the table. It was worth it. The last few hours with Grace had been nothing short of amazing. She was clever, intelligent, and had a unique perspective on just about everything. He wanted to ask her a million more questions. He also really wanted to kiss her. He'd been fantasizing about half a dozen ways he could steal a kiss before the night was through because her mouth was too tantalizing to resist.

As much as he didn't want to admit it, his brother might have been right. He liked Grace—he *really* liked her.

Grace picked up her purse and coat. "We should go."

"Let me help you." Ryan took her coat and opened it so she could slide her arms inside. When she turned to look up at him, those dark blue eyes cast a spell over him, and he was happy to be bewitched. Part of him warned that he was falling hard and fast for this woman, but he was in too deep to care. He put on his own coat, and they walked arm in arm out of the restaurant.

They crossed the parking lot and paused in front of her car, and a strange, boyish flutter of nerves buffeted his ribcage. She paused as she unlocked her car and peered up at him hopefully.

"I had a good time tonight," he said slowly, uncertain what to say after that.

"Me too."

"We could have a good time again soon." He realized too late the sexual suggestion in his words. "Shit, sorry, I didn't mean to say it like that."

Without a word, Grace stood up on her tiptoes and kissed him. His entire body turned into a live wire. Electricity shot through him, freezing out all rational thought. He basked in his own basic instincts. He grasped her waist, pinning her against the side of the car as he fought to get closer, to feel her body against his, his mouth devouring hers.

She tasted so damn sweet. He became drunk on the taste of her. Kissing her felt elemental, as if he'd been created solely to be hers, to kiss her, touch her, belong to her. A surge of possessiveness, of complete certainty that he was hers and she was his, stunned him. He had never felt so primal about a woman before in his life.

He wasn't sure how long their mouths moved together, but finally he came up for air. He still had her pressed against her car, his forehead resting against hers.

"Fuck, all I was going to do was ask you for your cell phone number, not maul you."

Grace still stared at his mouth hungrily, and then she grinned.

"I think I wanted a bit more than a number. I think . . . I think we should do this again. Soon." She rolled her hips ever so slightly over his, and he became painfully aware of how hard he was. More importantly, she wasn't referring to their date but what came after.

"Yes, *hell* yes, we should," he agreed gruffly. He was home for the next month, with no traveling needed for work. That left a lot of free nights open to spend with Grace.

She tilted her face up to his, her mouth ripe for another kiss, but as he leaned in, she suddenly stiffened. With a scream of warning, she shoved him sideways away from her. He flew nearly ten feet, tumbling on the asphalt.

"What the . . . ?" He groaned as he rolled onto his back and then struggled to sit up. Grace was still by the car, but something protruded from her stomach. It looked like an arrow. No, smaller than that. Something that might be fired from a crossbow.

"Grace!" He surged to his feet and sprinted toward her. But before he could reach her, someone knocked him to the ground.

A man in urban camouflage, holding a thin wooden stake, threw himself forward on Ryan, trying to stab him in the chest. Ryan somehow blocked the move with a swipe of his forearm and flipped his body so they rolled and he had the crazed lunatic beneath him.

"Goddamn bloodsucker!" the man snarled, his eyes filled with a hatred that made no sense.

"Ryan . . ." He heard Grace breathe his name.

Before the man could throw him off, Ryan swung a fist and clocked him hard, knocking him out cold. He sat back on his heels, panting as he clutched his bruised knuckles. He turned to Grace. She was pale, and her hands were tight around the arrow in her belly.

"Oh my God . . ." He got to his feet and rushed to her side before she crumpled to the ground. "Hang on. I'll call an ambulance."

"No!" Grace pleaded. "No, no doctors. No hospitals. You have to trust me. Take me to Jake and Georgie. Now." Her plea was so desperate his heart felt as if he had been the one to take the arrow, not her.

"Grace, you're bleeding bad. You need to go to a hospital."

"No, *no* hospitals," she growled, and the animal-like sound made him draw back a few inches, not from fear but concern. Her blue eyes were dark, but within seconds, they seemed to be rimmed with a red fire.

"Grace, you are really hurt. We have to take you—"

"Call Jake *now*. Tell him I'm hurt. He'll tell you what to do. *Do it*."

She leaned against the car door while Ryan dialed Jake's number, his hands shaking.

"Pick up, dammit," Ryan snarled into the phone.

When his brother finally answered with a chuckle of "Hey, little brother," Ryan cut him off.

"Grace is hurt. Some freak with a damn crossbow *shot* her. She's bleeding bad, and she won't let me take her to a hospital—"

"What?! No, do not do that. Listen carefully. Open her car, check everywhere for a small cooler. She needs what's inside. Do you understand? You'll also need to pull the arrow out."

"What?" Ryan inhaled sharply. None of this made any sense.

"Ryan, listen to me. Find the cooler. Bring her what's inside. Then remove the arrow. Put me on speaker so I can talk to Grace, then look for the cooler in her car. Go!"

Ryan put the phone on speaker and set it down close to Grace. She was so pale, her skin a white marble shade that was terrifying him.

"Jake's on speakerphone. Tell him what happened." Then he stood and went around to the passenger side of Grace's car and opened the door. A small travel cooler with a biohazard sticker on it sat on the floor. He opened the cooler and found . . . He didn't know what he'd expected to find. Some kind of medical kit, maybe? But the only things inside were four bags of blood, without any tubes or needles or anything else to help get the blood inside her.

Something in his brain was screaming for his attention, trying to warn him. But he wasn't listening. Everything was blocked out by the need to help Grace. Jake wouldn't have told him to do this if it wasn't important. He grabbed it and raced back around the car to Grace and knelt by her side. He heard his brother's tinny voice over the speaker.

"Grace, you have to tell him. Georgie and I are on our way. We'll meet you at Ryan's apartment, okay? Is he back yet?"

"I'm here." Ryan jumped into the conversation. "But the only thing in the cooler was blood. I didn't see any needles or—?"

"Don't worry about that. Lay her flat on her back and remove the arrow."

This was insane. Ryan knew from the first aid courses he'd taken that removing the impaling object was the *last* thing you were supposed to do. That was doctor work. "Jake, what's going on?"

"You always trusted me before, little brother. Trust me now."

Ryan laid Grace down and examined the arrow. It hadn't passed through her body, but he was afraid of how deep it went and if it had a hunting tip or something that would do more damage coming out than going in.

Grace put a hand on his arm. "Ryan, it's okay. Just get it out of me and I'll be okay."

The screaming in his brain became muffled. He stared into her eyes, which were now a dark crimson. In a daze, he nodded and then focused back on her wound. Without thinking, he gripped the arrow with one hand and held her stomach with the other and then pulled. She bit her lip and stiffened as he removed it. When it was free, he tossed it away.

Wait, had he really done that? That had to be a mistake. What had he done?

"Oh no. Tell me you're okay . . . *Please.*" He cupped her face with one hand.

"I need blood. Give me a bag and help me sit up," she said in a pained whisper.

Ryan lifted Grace to sit up again by the car, reached into the cooler, then held out the bag of blood. She took it and bit into the top of it with her teeth and began to drink.

Stunned, Ryan stared at her as the bag emptied before his eyes. She was *drinking* blood.

"Ryan?" Jake's distant voice came to the speaker. "Still there?"

Ryan lifted the phone and stared at Grace.

"Uh . . . yeah . . . I'm here," he said, his eyes never leaving Grace's face as she set the empty bag down and grabbed the next one from the cooler. She opened her mouth, and he glimpsed two elongated canine teeth the second before she bit into the bag. The screaming in his head had changed to a vague sense of "I told you so."

"Jake, she's . . . drinking the blood," he told his brother.

"Don't freak out on me, little brother, okay? Georgie and I will explain everything when we get to you."

"Yeah, sure, why would I freak out . . . ?" Ryan said absently while Grace finished the third bag before she leaned back against the car with a shaky sigh. "I'm sure this has a *perfectly* normal explanation."

"Just get Grace in the car and go to your apartment immediately," Jake said before he hung up. For a long second, Ryan stared at Grace. The crimson in her eyes had lessened somewhat.

"Tell me what the hell is going on," Ryan said. "This isn't normal. It's . . ."

"It's not," Grace agreed, and a century's worth of sorrow shone in her gorgeous eyes. "But when I tell you, you're going to panic. You're going to run."

Her gentle accusation made him stiffen.

"I'm not going to run, Grace."

She smiled ruefully. "We'll see."

"So tell me," he pressed.

She gazed at him a long moment, as if she might never see him again and wanted to burn him into her memory, as though he truly mattered to her.

"I'm not . . . human. Not anymore."

Her words didn't immediately register with him. "Not human?"

"Not human," she echoed, and then slowly widened her mouth, peeling back her lips like she was snarling, and he saw again more clearly those two long, sharp canine teeth in her upper jaw.

Fangs. They were fangs.

"I'm a vampire," Grace said.

A vampire. That made even less sense than her saying she wasn't human.

"What?" Ryan asked since no other response was possible.

Grace patted one hand on the lid of the cooler of empty blood bags.

"This isn't happening. This can't be real."

"I'm sorry, Ryan. I didn't want you to find out this way."

The signs were all there. The way she'd thrown him like a rag doll. The crazy goon's rant when he tried to stab Ryan. The blood in a cooler. The fangs. The fact that she was already starting to recover from being shot in the gut . . .

And yet his brain refused to accept what was happening.

"You . . . You're still hurt. We need a . . . doctor, or something. I should . . ."

"No, Ryan. No doctor. And you know why."

"Clearly, I don't know anything," Ryan blurted out. "Because everything I *thought* I knew just got blown out the window. Who are you? Who are you really?"

Grace sat up a little straighter. "Can we go to your apartment now? I need to rest until your brother and Georgina arrive."

Jake . . . Jake knew. Jake knew what was going on and hadn't told him.

"Ryan. I need you to focus. Listen to me carefully, okay? Your brain isn't lying to you. What you've seen really happened. I'm a vampire. And I need you to pick me up and help me into the car *right now.*"

Ryan's body seemed to act on its own while his brain still tried to process what she'd said.

He carefully lifted Grace to her feet, and she leaned against him as he took her to the passenger side of the car.

He helped her inside, then retrieved the cooler and put it in the trunk. He found Grace's keys and got into the driver's seat, but he was bent like a pretzel and was forced to adjust the seat so he could drive.

Grace gave an exhausted chuckle. "Sorry about that."

"It's fine. You're just so short," Ryan said.

"No, you're just so tall," Grace countered.

He drove the speed limit, but he was tempted to floor it to get to his apartment faster. All the while, he replayed the night's events in his head. The man who'd attacked them, shot Grace with a crossbow. What the hell had that been about? Then she drank blood and he'd seen fangs. And Jake . . . His brother knew about all of this. Knew what was going on . . . what she was.

Had Jake knowingly sent him on a blind date with a vampire?

FOUR

Grace could feel her stomach wound healing. The torn tissue and damaged organs were knitting themselves back together, but she needed more blood. *A lot more.*

Her mind and body silently screamed for more blood, and Ryan's warm-blooded scent was not helping her self-control. The heater in the car was blowing warm air and stirred the slightly curled ends of Ryan's hair at the base of his neck. He had gorgeous hair, and she wanted to dig her fingers into the dark silky strands while sinking her teeth into the pulsing artery of his neck. She licked her lips at the thought of how his blood would taste. A true mate's blood was an aphrodisiac to a vampire. She hadn't hungered for a man this much since William, and the thought was a poignant ache in her chest.

"How are you doing?" Ryan asked, and his innocent question broke through the not-so-innocent thoughts she was having.

"I'm hungry," she replied honestly, and then flinched. She was usually so good at acting human, but now that he knew what she was, it made it hard to be anything other than herself.

"Well, this isn't exactly Meals on Wheels." He chuckled wryly, clearly using humor as a coping mechanism, but she could hear how fast his heart was beating. He was anxious. How could she blame him? He was stuck in a car with a hungry vampire.

"Are you going to be okay until we get to my place?"

She almost laughed. "I'll be fine. How are *you* doing?" Ever since she had dropped the "V" bomb on him, she'd wondered if he'd go into full-on denial. It was amazing the things humans could convince themselves hadn't happened, even when they had seen it with their own eyes.

"You're bleeding out, and I can't take you to a hospital. *That* is freaking me out," Ryan admitted.

He parked the car in front of an upscale apartment building in a "Resident Reserved" spot and glanced around. Then, ever the gentleman, he came around to her side of the car and helped her out. His body heat was intensely warm, and it made the sweet scent of his blood intoxicating. Her fangs ached as they descended a little more, readying her to bite. She had to tamp down the instinct to lean in and just steal a little taste.

Ryan eyed her worriedly. "You're covered in blood. Anyone who sees you will freak out. You should take my coat. It will hide the blood, and we'll take the back elevators where we're less likely to be seen."

"Good thinking." She opened the car door, but he was already at her side, helping her to her feet. He quickly removed his coat and helped her put it on. Instantly his scent, embedded in the fabric, surrounded her, and heat lingered in the cloth where his body had warmed it. She shivered as she savored the feel of it. It was almost as nice as being held in his arms. She wanted nothing more in that moment than to be held . . . held while she fed on him. What would it feel like to have his strong arms caging her while she drank his equally strong blood? It would feel like nirvana.

He locked the car and put an arm around her from behind, helping her move. They looked rather like a young couple walking along romantically entwined, but the truth was she still needed his strength to move. The bags of blood she had consumed only covered her normal hunger as a vampire, the amount she would drink in about a week.

When that hunter had shot her, her body had gone into overdrive, stopping the wound, repairing the damage, but that took energy, and it would take far more blood to replenish her.

Hopefully, Jake and Georgie would be here soon, because Ryan's neck was looking like a glass of water in a very dry desert.

They entered the building through a back door and headed to the elevator bay. Ryan hit the top floor button, and soon they were heading up to his place. He put his arm around her shoulders, holding her close.

Poor human, he's too close, the predator in her couldn't help but think as she leaned in toward him. She caught a glimpse of their reflection in the gold-tinted mirrors of the elevator. Ryan was a tall, dashing, dark-haired man, his sweater slightly molded to his muscular shoulders and arms and loosening around his trim waist. She leaned into him, so small by compari-son, yet they fit—their bodies molded together easily in the light embrace he held her in.

What would it look like to watch herself feed on this gorgeous man in the mirror? Watch his head thrown back as she sank her fangs into his neck? He'd fist a hand in her hair, hold her closer, and groan . . . The fantasy was so strong, so close to becoming a reality that Grace moaned.

"You okay?" Ryan whispered and brushed his knuckles over her cheek.

"Yeah, I just need a minute." She shyly ducked her head, avoiding looking at the mirrors lest she lose that last thread of control.

The elevator doors opened, and they entered a short hallway with only one door. Ryan placed a black key fob against the lock and opened the door. He helped Grace inside, then took her to a large brown leather couch facing a big wall-mounted TV. The fireplace beneath the TV glowed with blue dragon glass stones.

"Sit here. Let me grab some towels and the first aid kit." He disappeared into a bedroom, and it gave Grace a moment to study his home.

It was definitely a masculine environment. All steel, wood, leather, and dark granite. She liked it. She had filled her own apartment with bright colors and light because it made her feel more human. But Ryan wasn't trying to be anyone but himself. She envied that more than she could say. His apartment felt warm and dark and intoxicating with that scent of his, which teased her nose and made her fangs ache. It was buried deep in every surface of this place, invisible to mortals, but not to her.

She removed Ryan's coat and held it up to her nose, drinking in his scent until she bit back a groan. She wanted to roll around in his bed naked, bathing herself in that scent. She wanted to . . . She wanted to climb his body and taste every inch of him. Then she wanted him to pin her down on that bed and take her the way a mate should—rough, wild, *primal.*

"Grace?"

Her eyes opened with a start, and she stared up at Ryan, her nose still pressed to his coat.

"We need to clean the wound, and I just need to see how bad it is." His voice deepened as he spoke, and he cleared his throat, making her fully aware that she'd been caught inhaling his scent like someone looking for a drug fix. But damn, she was *addicted* to his scent.

Completely mortified that she'd gotten caught sniffing his clothes, she lowered the coat to her lap and stared at the medical kit in his hands.

"I mean, I know you don't . . . work the same way we do. You seemed to have stopped bleeding before we even got inside, but still, I need to check. Are you okay with that?" For such a strong, ruggedly attractive man, he was rather adorable in his uncertainty.

"Okay." She didn't tell him that she didn't need the wound cleaned—infections only worked on the living —but she wouldn't mind getting out of her bloody blouse and skirt. Despite the fact that she was a vampire, she didn't *like* to be covered in blood like some wild barbarian.

"Come with me to the bathroom so I can get a better look."

Grace followed Ryan into his bedroom and then stepped into a large connected bathroom. The glass shower that took up one half of the room could hold ten people easily.

Ryan patted the white quartz countertop. "Sit up here, if you can." She stood on her tiptoes and eased onto the counter with his help. He was careful not to grab her waist, but instead lifted her almost like a child by grasping her under the arms. She blushed at how this mortal made her feel small and feminine in a way that appealed to every instinct that ran far deeper than her vampire nature. It was a human instinct, one that she thought had died long ago. Ryan reached for the top button of her blouse and cleared his throat, his gaze locked with hers.

"I think we should remove this. You want me to . . . er . . . ?"

"I can do it." She was more than a little afraid to let him undo her shirt. His touch on such a feminine part of her body would send her hunger into overdrive.

She slipped the buttons through her blue silk

blouse and peeled it off. She wore a fairly sensible cream bra that had a little bit of lace at the top, but she was still shy all the same. She *was* a modern-day vampire, but that old Victorian modesty still took hold of her at times, at least until her vampire hunger was too strong to ignore.

Ryan cleared his throat again. "Lean back, if it doesn't hurt too much."

She leaned back, bracing her hands on the counter. Ryan moved closer, and she parted her thighs a little, letting him stand between them as he dampened a cloth with isopropyl alcohol and then began to gently wipe the blood from her skin. She glanced down at the wound, which had sealed off and soon wouldn't even have a scar left behind. Her pale skin was a fiery red where it clenched around the closing wound.

"My God," Ryan breathed in wonder. His gaze moved up her body back to her face.

"I told you it would be all right, but I really need . . ."

She couldn't bring herself to say it, so he did it for her.

"Blood."

She lifted one leg up around his body, her foot hooking around his muscular thigh. It was getting harder and harder to ignore the predator inside her. She wanted to taste him. She wanted to *feed* on him.

"Grace," Ryan warned softly. She sensed fear, attraction, worry, desire.

She sat up slowly, curling her other foot around his leg and inching her skirt up to her hips as she pulled him closer. She didn't have to work hard to bring him to her—he was just as drunk as she was on the chemistry between them. Grace slid her hands up his chest and curled her arms around his neck. His hair fell into his eyes as he leaned in toward her. Their lips were mere inches apart now.

"Are you afraid?" She licked her lips and tilted her head another inch or so so that their mouths brushed, and his body tightened.

"Of you?" he asked in a husky reply.

"Yes."

Strength, lust, and something deeper buried burned in Ryan's eyes. For a moment, it seemed her vampire side was tamed, if such a thing was even possible. He fisted a hand in her hair.

"I'm only afraid of how much I *want* you."

She almost hissed a moment before their mouths merged in an explosive kiss. Everything seemed hazy and yet clear all at once as she tasted him. She savored his kiss the way she'd never savored anyone's except William's, and that had been more than eighty years ago. Those golden memories seem so terribly distant now, belonging to another life. Perhaps it *was* another life, another mate. She'd been given a second chance with Ryan, and she didn't want to let it go.

His lips traveled down her throat and bit teasingly before she could warn him not to. The playful bite triggered something in her. Grace burrowed her face in his neck and sank her fangs deep into him. Sweet, fiery blood hit her tongue, and she drew deeply on the vein that gave him life.

"Ahh," Ryan gasped, but rather than try to pull her away, he drew her closer just as she'd hoped.

He lifted her up in his arms, carrying her back into his bedroom, and soon she was lying on the bed with him. He pinned her beneath him.

Her mouth was still locked on his neck. She couldn't get enough. His blood was the most exquisite drug to her. It made her feel strong, wild. She dug her nails into his back, and he groaned and rocked his hips against hers, grinding against her core. The thin panties she wore were no barrier to the delicious friction of their bodies moving together. She wished she was a witch and could snap her fingers to make his clothes disappear.

She pulled her mouth away from his neck, licking her bloodstained teeth, and then she tugged at his sweater.

"Off," she growled.

Ryan's deep, rumbling laugh made her smile.

"Bossy little thing, aren't you?" he asked as he lifted his sweater over his head.

She rolled him onto his back and straddled him. He stared up at her, completely trusting her, still lost in the aphrodisiac pleasure of her bite. She could kill him and he wouldn't even try to stop her. But she wouldn't— she'd never killed a human and wouldn't start now, no matter how much his blood sang to her. He was a possible true mate to her. He was sacred.

Now that she had his blood pumping in her veins, her hunger was partially sated. She calmed down and rocked her body on his as she smoothed her palms up his chest. He was made of lean lines and hard muscles that bunched beneath her palms. He was a perfectly built man, and she wanted to taste every inch of him with her lips before she returned to his neck and drank again. He reached up and gripped her wrists. His pupils dilated as he stared at her in wonder.

"You're so beautiful it hurts," he murmured.

Hundreds of men had said those words before, captured by her vampiric glamour. They were blind to seeing the real her, but not Ryan. As her mate, he shouldn't be affected by that. He was seeing the most human version of her possible right now.

"Kiss me," she begged. "Make me remember what it means to be alive."

He flipped them so she was once again beneath him.

"Sorry," he whispered with a charming smile against her mouth. "I like being on *top*." He grasped her wrists and pinned her down onto the mattress. She could easily have flipped him back, but she liked this dominant side of his. This was what she needed from her mate, someone who took control of their pleasure so she could be herself and revel in the passion without having to think too hard. Ryan would be a wonderful mate.

Her mate. She had almost fully bonded with him. All he had to do was drink from her in return, just a taste of her blood . . . and they would be mated. The bond would deepen whenever he turned into a vampire.

But she couldn't ask that of him, not now. Despite his bravado, he hadn't yet fully processed her being a vampire, what it really meant. Their mate lust had robbed him of his good sense, and she was holding on to her own by a bare thread.

Ryan's mouth settled on hers, his kiss carnal and rough in a way that made her normally cool body burn. His tongue played with hers and his grip tightened on her wrists, making her moan and roll her hips in invitation for more. She trailed her mouth back to his neck, lightly sinking her teeth in again and sampling Ryan's blood and reveling how close it made her feel to him.

Then she realized they weren't alone.

RYAN SHOUTED IN SHOCK AS SOMEONE WRENCHED HIM OFF Grace. He was slammed into the back wall by the open bedroom door.

"Grace!" he bellowed when she screamed in fear. Someone was holding Grace down on the bed. *Georgie.*

"It's okay, Ryan. She's *okay*," Jake said to him. "But she can't be near you right now. Not until she's calmed down . . . Shit!" Jake grabbed his shoulder and chin, examining Ryan's neck. "She's already fed on you. I was worried this would happen. You're bleeding."

Ryan, still breathing hard, stared at his brother.

"What . . . what do you mean, *fed* on me? We were just kissing and . . ." He hadn't felt a thing, only a sensation of . . . *Wait, was that the bite?*

"Come with me. I need to look at your neck and see how bad it is. You might have to go to the hospital if she bit you too deep."

"But Grace—" He tried to shove his brother, but Jake didn't budge an inch.

"Listen. Grace is fine. Georgie is going to give her blood right now so she won't attack you again." Jake steered him into the bathroom and retrieved the medical kit from where Ryan had left it.

"She didn't attack me, Jake. We . . ." Ryan blinked slowly as the full weight of everything that had happened tonight finally sank in. "Oh God, someone did attack us, though. Grace was hit. I pulled an arrow out of her. But she's . . . she's a vampire, Jake!"

"I know," Jake replied, his expression grim. "Your memories are coming back now. That's what happens when the glamour wears off."

Ryan dragged his hands through his hair, tugging hard on the strands, needing to feel that pain so that it grounded him in reality again. "What do you mean?"

"Her vampire allure, or glamour. It's a sort of power vampires possess. When she needed the blood to heal, she was able to seduce you so she could bite you. It makes a mortal's memories fade for a time so they don't remember being bitten."

But Ryan hadn't felt anything on his neck—not a bite, anyway. He clamped his hand over the spot where Grace had been . . . Well, not what he'd thought she'd been doing.

"I never forgot anything—it just didn't seem to matter until a second ago."

Georgie's voice came from the other room. "Jake?"

"Yeah?"

"Grace is okay now. She's calmed down. She lost a lot of blood when she was hurt. She might have gotten a *bit* carried away is all."

"Grace—" Ryan tried to move toward the bedroom door, but he couldn't budge an inch. Jake still had him trapped against the wall.

"You stay right here," Jake growled. His hands were hard on Ryan's shoulders as he pinned him in place.

"Let go of me!" Ryan shoved back, but again his brother was as impassable as stone. Had he been working out? Jake had always been stronger than Ryan growing up, but now that they were both in their late twenties, the playing field had evened out when it came to their relative strength. Yet he couldn't even get his brother to shift an inch.

"Not until your head clears."

Ryan saw a hint of red appear in his brother's eyes. Jake's lips peeled back, showing a hint of fangs.

"What the fuck? Jake . . ." For the first time, Ryan uttered his brother's name out of fear.

"Shit, this is not the way I wanted to do this," Jake

muttered. He dropped his hands from Ryan's shoulders. "I had a whole speech prepared and everything."

"Jake . . . what's going on?"

Jake glanced toward the bedroom. "I know about Grace and what she is—because I am one too."

"You mean you're a . . ." Ryan didn't say the word.

Jake also avoided saying it. "Yeah."

"When? For how long?" Ryan asked. His ears started to ring as he faced his brother . . . a *vampire*.

"A year. It's a long story. Georgie saved my life. If it hadn't been for her, I'd be dead and you'd be alone. I couldn't let that happen, not after we lost Mom and Dad."

Georgie peeked her head out from the other room. "Is Ryan okay?"

Ryan stared at his brother before his gaze flicked to the doorway. "And Georgie is . . . ?"

"Yes, just like Grace."

"So you set me up on a date with a vampire!?" Ryan asked.

Jake rubbed the back of his neck and glanced away.

"We thought if we found someone you liked enough that maybe you'd want to turn like me."

"*Turn?*" Ryan couldn't say more than that for a long minute as he processed his brother's words and the weight of them.

"You have to trust me, Ryan. Whatever you think you know about vampires, it's all muddled up in superstition, half-truths, and misconceptions. It's not a Bram Stoker thing. Hell, and no, we don't sparkle. But there is a far bigger world than you can imagine out there, and we're just a part of it."

That snapped Ryan out of the fog of his shock, and his anger flared. "And how am I supposed to believe your side of things, huh?" His hand came away from his neck sticky, wet, and red. "Jesus Christ, she *did* bite me!"

"It's not that bad, little brother," Jake consoled. "Sometimes instinct takes over and—"

"She didn't take a bite out of your neck!"

Jake tried to explain. "She didn't get a chance to clot it before I pulled you off her. If she'd had a chance to lick the wound, it would have clotted rather quickly."

Lick the wound? Why did that both disgust him and turn him on at the same time?

"I don't know what's worse, you setting me up on a date so I won't die alone or that you set me up with a bloodsucking *vampire*."

Just then, Grace appeared in the doorway, clutching her bloody blouse protectively to her chest, her lips parted. The look on her face cut Ryan deep. She had heard everything he'd said.

"Georgie, I think it's time for me to go now." Grace fled out the door.

"Grace—" Ryan stopped and cursed bitterly. He had hurt her, deeply, but he hadn't meant to. He'd wanted to hurt his brother.

Georgie glanced between Ryan and Jake before she chased after Grace.

Ryan tried to follow, but Jake held his arm firm.

"I need to talk to Grace."

"Not yet. We have to talk, Ryan. There's a lot I need to tell you."

"Oh, you think?" Ryan crossed his arms over his bare chest and stared at his brother. "You have five minutes." He tapped his watch impatiently, and Jake, ever the older brother, glared at him before he began talking.

"It all started with the accident . . ."

FIVE

Jake finished telling his tale while applying a bandage to Ryan's neck. Somehow, despite all the evidence in front of him, part of his brain still tried to reject the truth. His brother was a *vampire*. His brother's fiancée was a vampire. Grace was a vampire.

Was anyone here *not* a damn vampire other than him?

"Ryan?" Jake said his name as though he expected Ryan to explode like a ticking bomb.

"What?" Ryan demanded.

"This is the part where you ask me questions."

Jake was right, he had a *lot* of questions, but every minute he wasted was one more minute Grace got farther away. He felt he had to apologize to her, if nothing else.

The image of that arrow protruding from Grace's chest flashed across his eyes. "Can you be killed?"

"Yes. Beheading, fire, not having enough fresh blood in our system."

"Those things kill normal people too, you know." Jake leaned against Ryan's bathroom counter, facing him. "I mean, what about the unusual stuff? Silver? Holy water? Sunlight?"

"Sunlight affects us, but it's not like we fry and turn to dust or anything," Jake chuckled. "But it makes most of us sleepy. The older you are, the less vulnerable you are to it. Right, Georgie?"

Ryan hadn't even heard Georgie come back. She joined them now, locking her arm through Jake's, and she brushed her dark glossy hair over her shoulder and leaned a little closer to Jake as she shyly met Ryan's hard gaze. Georgie had never been shy around him before, but it was clear she had not been ready for her vampire secret to be revealed to Ryan either. Maybe they had been waiting to see if there was a second date? Ryan tried to curb his anger at his brother for keeping something of this magnitude from him.

"The older a vampire is, the better they can withstand the sunlight. Most develop a resistance to it, some don't. It makes all of us vulnerable, though. The more we're exposed to it, the more we need fresh blood to stay in a healthy condition."

"And how much blood do you need to, you know, survive?"

"We really only need a few bags every week if we're being active and have no injuries. But we always travel with extra blood, like Grace did on her date with you. It's better to be safe than sorry."

"What, you don't just grab the nearest hitchhiker?"

Jake's eyes narrowed. Ryan knew part of him was trying to provoke his brother. He couldn't help it. But Jake continued to be patient with him. "Most don't risk that sort of thing, though it's not illegal among our kind to feed on humans," he added. "We have special blood banks that provide for us. Some vampires, of course, prefer to hunt the old-fashioned way, but it's easier to be noticed. It is illegal to kill humans, and once your fangs are deep in someone's neck it's easy to lose yourself and people get hurt . . . or killed. Blood banks then become the safest choice instead of feeding on humans."

"Oh, I expect the police love trying to solve those murders," Ryan muttered darkly.

Jake sighed. "We have to deal with the police and make them give up on the case. Of course, the Salem

Blood Society usually steps in and handles the vampires. They are dealt with according to our laws." Jake didn't explain what he meant, but Ryan supposed this wasn't the time for that. He tried to swallow down the sense of panic he felt at his own brother speaking of humans as if he wasn't one any longer.

"This glamour thing you mentioned, what is that? Vampire hypnotism?"

"Pretty much," Jake said. "It's also called vampiric allure. But we can't make you do anything you don't want to. More like it startles and stuns you, then you just sort of let go of your worries and concerns. It can also muddle your memory if a vampire bites you. It protects a human against the painful memory of our bite."

Ryan's hand reflexively went up to check the bandage. "And Grace did this when she fed on me tonight?"

"Yes, she needed more blood, and you were the closest source. Her instincts took over."

"But I remember *everything*, Jake. It was fucking amazing I . . ." He stopped himself from gushing about the heavenly feeling of kissing Grace and tried to put it into something more concise.

"She made me feel at peace," he said at last.

Jake and Georgie shared a look.

"At peace? Not buzzed like you'd been drinking?" Jake asked.

Ryan's frown deepened. "Well, yeah, I felt a level of euphoria and excitement too, but her kiss only made me feel happy. I felt completely and utterly at peace."

Georgie slowly smiled. "Guess I was right."

The haunted look in Jake's eyes began to fade. "You mean he's . . . ?"

"Oh yeah." Georgie was starting to bounce on her feet like a kid on Christmas morning, ready to open presents.

"Guys, stop that mind-reading bullshit. Wait, *can* you read minds?" Ryan hoped they couldn't, for a lot of reasons.

"What? No. What makes you say that?" Georgie asked with a laugh.

"Thank God for that. Now, what the hell are you so happy about?"

"It's possible that you're a true mate to Grace," Georgie explained.

"What's *that* supposed to mean?" Ryan asked. The word *mate* made him think of wolf packs or something, which then made him think of werewolves. *Oh crap, were werewolves real too?*

"A true mate is a mate nature creates only for you. I mean, they exist for everyone, but because we perceive things in such heightened ways, the experience is far more profound."

"What, only one? Like a once-in-a-lifetime thing?"

"Oh, there can be more than one possible mate out there, but it's hard to find even one. Mates are a gift."

Mates are a gift. The words echoed in his mind, and all he could think of was how he'd felt the moment he'd first seen Grace at the bar, how she'd felt like a gift, even before he knew that she was his blind date.

"It's what we were hoping would happen, Ryan. That you would find a vampire mate and that, when you were ready, you would turn," Jake said.

"Turn into a vampire . . ." Ryan couldn't believe they had circled back to that. His brother wanted him to turn into something supernatural, *un*natural, something that wasn't alive. At least, not in a normal way. Something about that, about Jake wanting him to make that sacrifice, to remove himself forever from the world he knew, hurt like hell. He also had a feeling that Jake wasn't telling him everything about vampires, and he was afraid to ask what his brother was holding back from him.

"Yeah," Jake said, his tone careful.

"You really think I'm a true mate to Grace?" Ryan still had no idea what that really meant, but he felt this was a conversation he needed to have with her in private once he had a better understanding of this whole situation.

"Sounds like you could be." Georgie was still smiling, but Ryan didn't share her enthusiasm. This sounded like a real commitment, something that continued past death. Until he talked to Grace, he wasn't going to agree to anything.

More importantly, he had no idea if he would ever want to turn into a vampire. He doubted Grace would be okay with that. He certainly wouldn't if their roles were reversed. He felt the weight of several huge decisions falling on him at once and didn't want to push himself into doing anything he would regret.

"Ryan?" Jake said his name calmly, but the tension in the room was thick.

"I need to see Grace. We need to talk. Georgie, can you give me her number and address?" If he couldn't catch up with her on the road, Ryan at least needed a way to contact her.

"Um, sure." Georgie pulled out her phone and texted him Grace's contact information. "Ryan, be gentle with her. She's pretty embarrassed about everything that happened tonight."

"Embarrassed about being shot in the chest by some nutjob?"

"What, that? No," Georgie replied. "It's just been a

long time since she's done the whole dating thing . . . and she got a little excited after she tasted you."

A long time. The thought made Ryan's head hurt. "How long?"

"Well . . . that's something she should share with you."

He sighed. "Fine. But I've got to go." He passed his brother and Georgie to retrieve his sweater and put it back on. Then he paused and looked back at them.

"This guy with the crossbow. I knocked him out in the parking lot of the Magic Pan. He was waiting for us, so he must have been tracking her. I'm sure he's gone by now, but we need to find him and, I don't know, do whatever we can to protect Grace from him. I have a feeling she's still in danger."

A low hum of warning had been building in his chest ever since they'd been attacked, but he was only just realizing what that feeling meant. He'd felt it when they left the restaurant, but he'd been so preoccupied about getting Grace's phone number that he'd assumed the feeling was just nerves.

"We'll look for him. Hunters in the area around Boston and Cauldron Falls are really uncommon. This guy was more than likely some wannabe hunter rather than the real deal. There are other ways our kind deals with those who attack vampires unprovoked. We have people we can ask to help us," Georgie soothed. "I'm sure Grace will be fine."

"We brought your car back by the way," Jake said.

"Thanks." Ryan shot his brother one more hard look before he grabbed his keys and left. Jake had a spare key, so they could let themselves out when they were ready. All that mattered to Ryan right now was finding Grace.

GRACE WAS AN ABSOLUTE WRECK. IT HAD BEEN A *REALLY* BAD night. Her blind date had been a possible true mate, and then she'd learned he didn't like her. She was just another bloodsucking vampire to him, straight out of some cheesy horror movie. Her mate . . . *hated* her.

Grace pulled over at a gas station at the next exit she came upon halfway between Boston and Cauldron Falls. She put her car in park and then buried her head in her hands and trembled as she fought off waves of grief and shame.

Being a vampire should be easy. Seduce her prey, drink, and be merry. But she'd never liked feeding on humans.

Until the vampire communities around the world had become organized and found a way to make bagged blood more easily available, feeding had just been another irritation of her immortality. A necessity. It could be enjoyed, yes, but it was never real, always fleeting, and once finished, soon forgotten by the prey.

But tonight, when she had fed on her true mate, she'd felt both power and peace at once. She'd felt as if she could do anything, as long as Ryan was with her. She'd bonded to him too quickly, but that was the way it was with true mates. They were a gift because you had no doubt they were made to be yours and no one else's.

Rain began to fall, misting the windows of her car. She stared through the patterned raindrops at the gas station's fluorescent lights. She was still hungry. She didn't need to hunt; she could make it back to her apartment and drink more blood there. But after feeding on Ryan, she still had this unsatisfied instinct to feed on prey that she could catch. She hadn't felt that urge in a long time, the need to hunt . . . She used her heightened vision and hearing to focus on the customers inside the shop.

She so often repressed her enhanced senses that now she had to focus on hunting . She could hear every heartbeat and all the different breaths. What she didn't notice was the figure outside her car until it suddenly loomed over her side window. She screamed, thinking for a moment that the goddamned hunter had tracked her down, when the man wiped an arm on the window, letting her see his face.

"Ryan?"

"Grace, please, we need to talk." He walked around to the passenger side of her car, and she hit the unlock button for the doors. A moment later, he slid into the passenger seat and closed the door. The scent of him hit her hard, the scent of man and rain. Those two aromas blended sweeter than any wine bouquet she'd ever inhaled.

"How did you find me?" she asked.

"Georgie has the Find My Friends app on her phone, and she told me you'd stopped here."

"Oh . . ." She was always forgetting how smart technology was.

He dragged a hand through his rain-soaked hair and faced her, clearing his throat.

"What I said back there . . ."

His eyes held hers, and she wanted to crawl into his lap and sink all of herself into him. Whatever he was going to say next would hurt, but she could handle it. She'd have to.

"It's okay, Ryan. I *am* a bloodsucking vam—"

He placed a fingertip on her lips. "No, you aren't. I mean, you *are*, but I was really pissed at my brother for keeping this all a secret. It wasn't aimed at you. Still, it's inexcusable. If my mother was still alive, she would kill me." He smiled ruefully. "Point is, I didn't act like a gentleman. I acted like a jerk. I know you're a vampire, but I don't think you're a bloodsucking monster of the night."

Grace offered a sad smile. "You just found out that your brother is a vampire. That's a huge shock."

Ryan slowly reached for one of Grace's hands, which rested in her lap. She didn't pull away. She craved his touch too much.

"Georgie gave me the talk. Well, her and Jake. I still have a million questions, but right now, we need to get you somewhere safe. Whoever attacked you tonight knew where you'd be. They might try to find you again. I have an idea, but you'll have to trust me."

Trust him? It would have been harder *not* to trust him, but her real concern was that neither of them knew exactly what they were facing.

"I'm listening."

"Leave your car here tonight. We'll take my car, find a motel off the main roads. Then we can talk about all this."

"You're so calm," she couldn't help but say. Any

other mortal would have still been in shock or would have firmly transitioned to panic.

"This isn't the first time I've had my life turned upside down. I've got a surprisingly good hold on my reactions. Yes, the whole vampire thing and my brother now being one threw me off, but the more I know, the more I can come to grips with this."

He stroked his thumb against her wrist, and her heart, unalive as it was, seemed to quiver with a very human longing.

"Okay. So where are we going?"

Ryan's lips kicked up in a crooked grin that made her knees weak. "There's a cozy little motel not far from here. I thought we could talk about everything."

"Just talk?" she asked, unable to hide her own hope-fulness.

"Well, maybe more than that, but only if you want to."

"Okay," she agreed with a hesitant smile.

Grace let him take her to his Range Rover, and he opened the door for her. The rain was coming down harder than ever, but the cold didn't really register with her. Ryan, however, was cold and shouldn't be. She reached over and turned on the car heater as Ryan wiped rain from his eyes.

"Thanks," he said, offering a soft smile.

"No problem." She remained quiet and so did he until they reached a small but nice one-story motel.

"Stay here. I'll get us a room." Ryan came back a few minutes later with a room key. "Our room is around back. That way, no one will see my car from the road, assuming that creep who attacked us knows what kind of car I'm driving."

That creep. He meant the man who'd shot her. The vampire hunter. She'd had run-ins with supernatural hunters before, long ago, but usually it had been because she'd been caught feeding on someone. But she hadn't fed on a human in ages, and she hadn't fed on Ryan tonight until after the attack. So what had caused the hunter to come after her? How did he know where she was?

Her brain stuttered to a sudden halt.

"Gabriel," she breathed.

"What?" Ryan parked in front of room number eight on the back side of the hotel.

"I was trying to think about what I did that gave me away to a vampire hunter tonight, and I couldn't think of anything until . . . Gabriel."

"The asshole we ran into at the Magic Pan?" Ryan connected the dots quickly. "You think he ratted you out?"

"Yes."

"I should have decked him when I had the chance." He seemed to consider what might have happened if he had. "Wait, he's not a vampire too, is he?"

"No, but he's not human either. Well, he is, but he's also a warlock, so he's technically from the supernatural world like me. Punching him would have been a mistake."

"Ahh. That explains what he said. He mentioned something to you about dating in the super world. You also said he was toxic."

"You have *no* idea."

"Let's get inside and you can tell me everything."

Grace followed him into the cozy little room. He locked the door and slid the extra bolt into place, as if that would keep out all the bad things in the world. It was sweet that he had such confidence in a simple lock. A vampire could easily kick that door down, or command him to open it himself since it wasn't soundproof, but she didn't dare tell him that.

Ryan pulled the curtains closed on the solitary window before he turned on a light in the room. Grace perched delicately on the end of the only bed in the room. Ryan came over and placed his hands on her shoulders.

"You're freezing," he murmured in concern.

She gave a little shrug. "It doesn't bother me. I don't feel heat the way you do."

"Right." A slight crease formed between his brows. "You're still wet, though. That can't be good."

"We don't get sick either." Well, not completely true, but true enough for the moment.

"Yeah, but still." He went into the bathroom and retrieved a large bath towel and started to wrap it around her. His eyes brightened. "Hang on." He left the room, and she heard him rummaging around in his car before coming back inside the room. He carried a small leather weekender bag over one shoulder.

He dropped the bag beside her and dug through the contents until he pulled out a thick plaid flannel shirt that buttoned up. He chuckled. "I swear these are clean. I always do laundry the day before I leave to come home on a trip in case I get stranded somewhere and need fresh clothes. I forgot I even had these in the back of my car. Is this okay? To wear tonight, I mean?"

Grace accepted the shirt with a shaky smile. "It will be perfect for all the wood chopping I need to do," she teased.

"I know, I dress like a lumberjack when I hit the colder climates for my job." He shrugged out of his drenched overcoat and removed his sweater, baring his chest. When he turned his back on her to change, she saw the red score marks her nails had made on his back when they'd been kissing on his bed. It embarrassed her and thrilled her to see the marks on him. She worked so hard to ignore the vampire side of herself, the side that wanted to shout in sweet triumph at leaving a possessive mark on her mate.

"You . . . should shower. You've got to be freezing," she observed.

Ryan chuckled. "I tend to run a little hot, but I'm happy to shower if you want to watch. Or better yet, join me."

She arched her brow at him. "I thought you wanted to talk about all this first?"

Ryan smirked. "We can always talk after."

"Are you sure it's not you who's the vampire?" she asked, half-serious. He had all the flirtatious dark charm that made her kind extremely seductive.

Ryan knelt on the floor in front of her, and with his height, it brought them practically eye to eye.

"Maybe it's crazy, but I have this desire to jump all-in with you," he murmured as he cupped her face.

"That's because we're—" She halted, not daring to say the words. It might scare him off.

"True mates?" he said, as if he could read her mind. "I don't really know what that is yet, but I want you to tell me, maybe even show me, what that means."

He was so smooth, so seductive as he stood and lifted her to her feet. Before she could even realize what was happening, he was leading her to the shower. She felt like a young woman of twenty all over again, an innocent damsel who had been seduced and turned in a dark alcove beneath the back stairs of an English manor house.

But that had been against her will. This time was different. Grace knew Ryan would listen if she said *no* or *slow down* or *stop*. But the truth was, she wanted to go fast. She wanted to jump, just like Ryan did, into this madness. She wanted the sweet abandon of being loved and cherished in her mate's arms.

Ryan turned on the water, and steam began to fill the bathroom and fog the mirror. He crooked one finger at her in silent invitation to join him.

She was unable to resist him. She went straight into Ryan's arms, ready for whatever came next. She hungered for him in a way she had never hungered for anything else.

Grace let him undress her bit by bit, slowly baring her skin until she was only wearing a bra and panties. He, by contrast, still had on his jeans, boots, and socks. She slid a finger into the belt loop of his jeans and pulled him toward her. She may be a modern woman now, but there would always be a part of her that felt like an innocent Victorian maiden when it came to desire. She wanted to be chased, wooed, and seduced *thoroughly*. Thankfully, Ryan made it easy for her to be herself and to be open about her desires, both vampiric and human.

His hands, so blissfully warm on her skin, roamed over her shoulders, arms, and then down to the flare of her hips. He traced the now faint pink scar where an hour ago she had been pierced by an arrow.

"Does it still hurt?" He gazed down at her, those mesmerizing brown eyes so gentle, yet she saw a wealth of desire burning steadily within them.

"Not anymore." She would have pulled away from anyone else's touch out of pure instinct, but with Ryan, she had to keep herself from demanding he touch her more, *everywhere.*

"That's incredible." His hands drifted lower toward the top of her panties. He played with the lace that lined the top, and a throbbing need started between her thighs.

"You're still cold," she said, even though she was the one who shivered. "You should get in the shower and warm up."

"Only if you join me." He dropped his hands from her body and toed out of his boots, then unzipped his jeans and tugged them down. He wore a pair of green-and-black boxers, and when he tugged those down too, she saw the V-shaped indentations that pointed down to . . . *Oh my.* He *was* well endowed, wasn't he?

"Come on." He turned his back to her, and she was treated to a view of his firm buttocks as he stepped into the shower. She wanted to clench his ass and feel those muscles move as he pounded into her.

Grace stifled a moan as the throb between her thighs turned to a sharp ache.

His commanding tone, while playful, stirred her feminine side. When she was with a man she trusted, domination in bed could be exciting, because she knew she still had control. Ryan gave her that comfort and trust instantly. She hastily shed her bra and panties and joined him in the shower. He pulled the curtain closed, sealing them in a cocoon of warmth.

"Come here, little vampire," he teased with a grin and pulled her into his arms, hugging her as if they had been lovers for centuries and not strangers who'd met only a few hours ago.

This was the part of true mates that she had forgotten. This easy feeling of acceptance, trust, and mutual desire. She and William had shared this too, but those memories were hazy now, as if they'd happened to someone else. So many of her past memories had been buried by the trauma of Gabriel's spells.

"This is nice," she whispered against Ryan's chest.

"It is, isn't it?" he admitted. "I'd forgotten how good it feels to have someone I care about in my arms."

The hot water cascaded over them. He had forgotten what it felt like to hold a woman? It made her wonder about him, about his past, and she felt safe enough right then to ask.

"How long has it been since you've dated?"

"I was involved with someone a few years ago. It

was pretty serious. Three years. I know that must not sound like much to you, but to me it was a long time."

"What happened?" She watched the water trail over his body and cling to his hair. A few defiant strands curled beneath the water, and she wanted to reach up and run her fingers along those rebellious curls. For some reason that made her smile.

"We cared about each other, but realized there was no real love. What we'd thought was love was just desire, and one day that was gone. Then we were just two people living as roommates. It felt so hollow. There was no nasty breakup or anything, just a mutual parting of ways. Still, it made me doubt myself, like, what if I ever only feel lust and can't tell if there is something deeper, you know? I didn't want to make that mistake again."

"So what made you agree to a blind date?" she couldn't help but ask.

"Honestly? It was your voice. At least, I think I heard your voice. You were talking while Georgie was on the phone with me. Something about it just pulled me."

She knew what he meant. The first time she'd heard him speak at the bar, before she'd known he was her date, his voice had been like a glass of scotch, warm and slightly rough. She could have listened to him talk about anything.

"Do all vampires have the ability to do that with their voice?"

She shook her head. "Vampire allure only works in person," she said. "And it's a conscious thing."

"Then it must be the true mate thing, right?"

"Did Jake tell you about it?"

"Not everything. Georgie and Jake gave me a crash course, but they didn't go into a ton of detail because I needed to find you."

"So you know that this thing between us . . ."

"Goes both ways?" He sounded hopeful. "So you feel it too? It's like you're a magnet, drawing me toward you."

"It's the same for me. That's why I got a little carried away when we were at your apartment. I was lost in the mate passion."

"Georgie figured that must be it. Jake thought you just needed blood."

"Jake still has a lot to learn about being a vampire. I did need blood, but you being a possible mate actually made it safe for you to be around me."

"What do you mean?" His lips quirked in a half smile. They were completely naked in the shower, embraced so intimately, and yet they talked like they were on a date at a coffee shop.

"Our instincts drive us to protect our mates. We

wouldn't do something that would put them in danger, especially from ourselves."

"So when you kissed me . . ." His hands on her lower back traced patterns with his fingertips as he waited for her to finish his sentence.

"It was because I *wanted* to kiss you. It wasn't about blood."

A hint of tension he must have been holding on to faded away, and that wicked glint of sensual mischief was back in his eyes. "Good, because I want you to do it again."

"Bite you?"

He stared at her mouth. "I want you to *kiss* me, and then I want to take you right here in the shower, then again on the bed, and as many times as it takes until we collapse."

She liked the sound of that far too much. She bit her bottom lip, knowing one of her fangs was showing. He didn't recoil, however. Instead, he leaned in. Ryan cupped her face in his hands, and his mouth feathered over hers. The man knew just how to tease her. She parted her lips to his tongue, and just like that, the world burned.

She was consumed by his heat. He groaned and pulled her close until their bodies were pressed together from head to toe. The hard length of his shaft nudged against her belly, and she trembled with excitement and need. It had been too long since she'd been under the delicious sway of true passion. She blacked out the dark memories of nights with Gabriel. There was only this man, the hot water on her body, and the sweet fire of his kisses.

Ryan lifted her up by the waist, and she grasped his shoulders and wrapped her legs around him. She giggled against his lips.

"What?" he chuckled in response.

"I *climbed* you like a tree," she said, giggling again. "That was my thought when I first met you. I wanted to climb you and do this." She lifted herself up, rubbing herself against him. He responded with a deep growl that would have rivaled a werewolf and pinned her against the shower wall, then slowly thrust his cock inside her.

"You mean you wanted to do *this*?" Ryan asked in a low, gruff voice that made her clench tight around his shaft.

"Yes," she gasped. "*That.*" She arched her back, trying to get closer. "Did you want . . . to do this too?"

He withdrew from her. "Oh yeah, I fucking wanted to, so bad." He surged back in. "Just like this." He rolled his hips and hit a spot deep inside her that made her see stars.

He pumped deep several times, then quickened his pace, as if he wanted to find the right angle and rhythm. But all of it felt amazing. Heat raced between their bodies, and for a brief moment she felt human, *truly* human again. Her vampiric hunger was quelled. It was still there in the back of her mind, but silent. All she felt was unimaginable peace.

Her mate made love to her, and the intoxicating mix of rough loving and tenderness shook the very foundations of her soul. She cupped his jaw, feeling the slight scruff there when she kissed him, open-mouthed and raw. It sent them both racing toward a glorious peak of sensations. She was climbing a mountain, knowing that at any moment she would reach the top and fly off to the clouds far below.

Ryan thrust harder, faster, and she couldn't resist any longer. She sank her teeth into his neck, and that exquisite blend of blood and sex sent her rocketing over the edge. She was free-falling in sheer pleasure. Ryan's hoarse cry followed hers a moment later, and then they were drifting together, like two downy feathers caught upon a breeze, twirling and floating around each other.

He held her in his arms for a long moment before they finally separated. Grace immediately missed the connection of their bodies, but she hadn't lost that sense of closeness to him emotionally. Their bonding was beginning.

"That was . . . Fuck, I can't even say what that was. *Incredible* seems inadequate." He pulled her close again and feathered a kiss against her brow.

Grace smiled. She knew exactly what he meant. *Incredible* seemed like such an insignificant word for what they'd just experienced.

They turned the water off. Ryan got out first, wrapping a towel around his waist, then holding a fluffy towel to her. She stepped out and he wrapped it around her body. She then accepted the long flannel shirt he'd previously offered. It felt oddly sexy wearing nothing but his shirt as she padded to the bed on bare feet and pulled back the covers. She wasn't tired—it was night, after all—but she was unbelievably relaxed. She wanted to lie in bed beside Ryan, feeling warm, safe, and cherished. She closed her eyes, intending to rest and nothing more, but sleep came surprisingly fast.

WHEN RYAN CAME BACK OUT OF THE BATHROOM, HE PAUSED to admire the sight of Grace asleep in bed. So vampires did sleep, or did something like it. His lips twitched as he took in the way his red flannel shirt enveloped her curvy little body. Maybe it was his inner caveman talking, but he loved seeing her in his clothes. It made him feel like he was caring for her. Granted, she was a vampire and could take care of herself, but that didn't mean he didn't want to try. He couldn't get the image of her hurt and bleeding out of his mind. He felt compelled to protect her, throw himself in the path of danger, even if it put his life at risk.

It probably should have shocked the hell out of him to feel so protective of her, but it felt so natural. That had to be the true mate thing at work. He wondered if it worked both ways, or if he was simply under her spell. That took his mind to some dark places. Perhaps it was how vampires protected themselves, having humans devoted to their survival.

Ryan shook his head. No, the rational part of his brain kept looking for all the ways this could go wrong, but his heart told a more convincing story. He moved quietly around the room and changed into a pair of pajama pants, then turned off the light and eased into bed beside Grace. She rolled to face him, cuddling up to him. Her body was cool, but not cold. He didn't mind since he always seemed to feel hot when he slept.

"What are we going to do?" he asked the sleeping vampire in his arms.

Grace stirred and rubbed her cheek against his bare chest. He brushed the hair back from her face and smiled like a fool. He reached over and picked up his phone from the night table and sent Jake a text, letting his brother know that he had found Grace and they were safe. Jake texted back saying he and Georgie were trying to track down the hunter who'd attacked them and he'd call as soon as he had any news.

For a long while, Ryan lay awake, comforted by holding his woman in his arms. But his mind refused to settle and ran over everything that had happened in the last few hours. He kept coming back to Jake. His brother was a vampire. Jake was *dead*. Well, undead. And he hadn't told Ryan.

Jake had been a vampire for a whole year and Ryan hadn't known. Why had he gone through something so huge without telling his own brother? Had Ryan been so wrapped up in his own solitude since he and Mandy had broken up that he'd lost sight of his relationship with his own brother?

He tightened his hold on Grace, fearing he'd somehow lose her too.

"Ryan?" Grace murmured his name and lifted her head to look at him. "You okay?"

"Sorry, I was just thinking."

"About Jake?"

"How did you know?" He trailed his fingertips over her jaw and tucked a lock of her hair behind her ear. "Is it a psychic thing?" He was teasing, of course, but she seemed to take his question seriously.

She shook her head. "He's your brother. Georgie told me it's been just the two of you since your parents died. His turning was a big secret that he kept from you, and it gnawed at him. I can only imagine how you must feel."

His throat tightened. For a moment he couldn't speak. "Why . . . I mean, *why* didn't he tell me? He died and I didn't even know."

"He got better." Now she was the one teasing him.

Ryan looked at her with narrowed eyes. Grace smiled sadly. "You're thinking of death in a permanent way. But when mortals turn into vampires, it's not a permanent death. Think of it like a change. His heart can still beat, it still pumps blood through his system. He can still breathe, but he can go without air if needed. It's just . . . *different*."

"It's not about that. You have to understand, we used to be *close*. I don't know who I'm more pissed at, him for not telling me or me for not noticing." He slid his hand down Grace's back, comforting himself. "I feel like I let him down somehow."

"You didn't. It's amazingly easy for mortals to not notice someone's change, especially if they have help. Jake had Georgie to guide him through his transition, which made it easier for him to look and feel more mortal to you."

"How did you turn, Grace?" he asked after another moment of silence. Even though he loved her voice, her silences were somehow calming. It gave him time to sort through his thoughts.

"I was at a ball when I was twenty."

"A ball? What year?"

"1883." She bit her lip, exposing her fangs again, and as weird as it was, he found that strangely adorable. It seemed her fangs only showed when her emotions were running high.

"So you're more than a century old?"

She nodded. "I turned a hundred and sixty last month."

"Shit..."

"Am I too old for you?" she teased, but her body stiffened, betraying how worried she was about his answer.

"Doesn't bother me, babe. I like my vampires aged like fine wine. *You,* on the other hand, are a cradle robber." He winked at her, hoping to win a smile. He wasn't disappointed.

"You are such a flirt," she chuckled.

"So you were at a ball . . ."

"It was in London. A big, lavish affair at a house owned by a friend of my parents. I was two years on the shelf by then and didn't expect to dance much."

"On the shelf?"

"It means that I was considered old, *undesired*, so I was put back on the proverbial shelf like a piece of unwanted merchandise."

Ryan frowned. "What kind of fucked-up bullshit is that?"

"Victorian fucked-up bullshit," Grace said with an adorable frown.

"Hearing you curse is kind of cute," Ryan admitted. "Okay, so what happened at the ball? Did a charming Dracula show up?"

She traced her index finger over his pectoral muscles as she smiled sadly.

"Kind of. There was a man, tall, dark, and beautiful. He swept into the room, and there was something magnetic about him."

"His glamour?" Ryan said grimly.

"Yes, not that I knew what that was until much later. He was hunting for a mate, and he felt the easiest way was to taste the blood of a woman. He sampled every young woman discreetly. I was his last taste."

"Were you his mate?"

She shook her head. "Dawn was an hour away, and he was ready to sleep. But he wanted a full meal before that. He'd simply been sampling women all night, just tiny pricks here and there, so he was still hungry. But when he lured me into the dark alcove beneath the servants' stairs, he had every intention of draining me. Killing me."

Grace shivered, and Ryan rubbed her back again, wishing he could do something to make her feel safe while she relived this moment in her mind.

"I was powerless against him, of course. He wasn't rough, he held me gently, but it wasn't out of kindness. More like etiquette. I was almost gone, and I remember gazing into his eyes, feeling such fear and helplessness, wishing that I could live. I thought about all the things I wished I could do, and perhaps he saw some of that as he fed.

"Whatever the reason, something made him pity me. He bit his wrist and forced his blood down my throat. He left me alone in a broom cupboard by the stairs, abandoned as I turned. I don't know what he was thinking, because without someone to guide them, a new vampire is most likely going to go feral, surrender to their animal instincts. Those vampires tend not to live very long.

"When I passed through the turn a few hours later, my body was desperate for blood. I attacked a scullery maid who came to collect her ash bucket for lighting the morning fires. Thankfully, I didn't kill her, but I would have if Georgie hadn't found me at that moment."

"Georgie was already a vampire?"

"Yes, she was turned a hundred years before me. She heard the maid's cries and stopped me from taking her life. I was so scared, so new, so *hungry*, and she took me in. I learned how to hunt without killing and how to use my new abilities. But I also needed to leave my old life forever."

She grew quiet at this point, then continued. "Georgie made it as painless as she could. For a time, we maintained the facade that everything was normal. She was posing as a lady at that time and got to know my parents. Eventually, she convinced them to let me leave London and travel with her as her companion. I corresponded with them by mail, but I never went home again until they died. It made things easier that way."

Ryan could see she was hurting, even after all this time. He felt her pain as though it was his own.

"I'm sorry," he whispered.

"For what?" she asked just as quietly.

"I'm sorry that I wasn't there back then, to be there for you." He meant it. He would have given anything to go back in time and simply be there for her when she needed someone to comfort her.

Grace slid over his body, straddled him, and leaned down to kiss him. It was the kind of kiss that made him feel as though he was connected to all things going back to the moment that light and energy burst forth in the universe. It was more than just a kiss. It was a glimpse into exquisite *infinity*.

He held her tight as she wriggled insistently above him. Understanding what she wanted, he shoved his pajama pants down a few inches to free his shaft. She took him with one hand and guided him inside her. They both shared a sigh as he sank into her, the connection between them impossibly deep, both physically and emotionally. Grace rode him leisurely, and their gazes locked and held. They didn't speak with words, but with their bodies. He held her hips, bathing in the rising pleasure of their lovemaking.

When he came deep inside her long minutes later, he cried her name like a fervent prayer and she clung to him, her eyes glowing with a supernatural light. He knew then he wasn't falling in love with her—he'd already fallen. It was that fast. It was almost instant, given that they'd only met each other a few hours ago, but he had shared so much of himself that he had never shared with anyone else before. She had done the same with him. There was something between them that wasn't just physical or chemical. The bond between them was deep. *Ancient.* A bond that had been born when the molten core of the earth first burned to life.

"I'm all in, Grace," he murmured. "I'm yours. I'm yours."

She gazed up at him, eyes wide with such a bright and burning hope that it was hard to breathe as love and that far softer pang of longing squeezed his chest.

"I'm yours too," she echoed. "I'm all in."

He dove into the fathomless depths of her blue eyes, forgetting all his worries for the moment. There was just her in this private universe.

Grinning like a fool, he cupped her face and kissed her again, eager to get lost in her over and over again.

"What do you mean, you *killed* the female?" Gabriel demanded.

"I got her with an arrow. Right in the heart." The hunter tapped his chest proudly, but the effect was somewhat lessened by the bag of frozen peas he held against his bruised face. "That bloodsucker is dead. But I didn't get her mate. The bastard knocked me out."

Gabriel held back the snarl of rage that surged in his throat. Grace couldn't be dead. That wasn't what he'd wanted. He'd wanted that *human* to be dead and for her to be injured so he could swoop in and rescue her. He'd wanted her to remember how well he'd cared for her when they'd been together. And this fool had failed on both counts.

"You saw her die?" Gabriel demanded. They both sat once again in the dingy little pub in the shadows, as they had when he'd recruited him.

"There's no way she could have survived." The hunter's voice brimmed with confidence, despite the pathetic way he held the frozen bag to his face. "She turned to dust while I was knocked out."

Gabriel closed his eyes tightly, willing himself to find his last bit of control. Turned to *dust*? This man was no hunter. He had gotten his knowledge of vampire lore from *television*.

That meant Grace had been removed from the scene, likely by the human male or other vampires. The matter was not yet closed. After a moment, Gabriel opened his eyes and found the stupid hunter still staring at him. A loose end now.

He reached into his pocket and pulled out a small leather hex bag.

"Your payment."

He emptied the contents into his hand, and the hunter leaned forward to stare at the mixture of magical ingredients.

"What's that supposed to—?"

Gabriel blew the contents right into the man's face.

The hunter coughed. "What the—?" Then his face suddenly turned blank.

"I think you have somewhere to be, don't you?" Gabriel intoned smoothly, but he was still boiling inside with rage.

The hunter dropped the bag of peas and stood. With a glazed look over his face, the man left the bar. A moment later, tires screeched, a car horn blared, and then the sound of a terrible crash shook the grubby little bar. Some of the patrons went outside to see what had happened.

Gabriel dusted his hands of the remaining hex powder and then reached into his coat pocket to find a small crystal orb he used for scrying.

"Show me Grace's last moments." He channeled his magic into the orb, focusing on Grace in his mind.

The orb clouded over, and he peered deeply into its milky center. He glimpsed Grace lying on top of the human man, kissing him, riding him to bliss and crying out in pleasure. These were her last moments . . . But Gabriel noticed the orb didn't go dark, the visions continued, showing Grace lying in the man's arms, smiling. If she'd truly been dead, the images would have stopped by now.

But they hadn't, because Grace was alive.

SEVEN

"What is it like?" Ryan asked Grace in a soft voice.

They were cuddled in their bed at the motel as dawn crested the horizon.

He felt a little guilty about keeping her awake when the sun was clearly making her so tired. But she was rather adorable while drowsy, like a sleeping kitten in his arms.

She knew what he was asking, but she danced around the words. Grace yawned and nuzzled his shoulder with her cheek. "What is what like?"

He drew in a deep breath. "Being a vampire. I want to understand what my brother went through. What it's like for him now."

He didn't want to say that he wanted to know

because his whole reality had shifted and he was still trying to catch up. All this had been the stuff of myth and movies twenty-four hours ago; now it was part of his world. And if he was a true mate to Grace, well, wouldn't he have to turn at some point? How could he die of old age and let her go on without him? Wasn't that selfish?

Of course, a lot of that depended on what the actual rules of life and death were amongst these people, and he still had no idea.

"You have heightened senses. Better vision and hearing, even a better sense of smell. But there is a hunger inside you that is never quite sated, and that makes you dangerous. But you learn to control it, for the most part." She yawned again.

"And turning? How does that work?"

She lifted her head, hope shining in her eyes. "Are you . . . are you thinking of turning?"

He couldn't deny her the truth, not when she was looking at him like he was a knight of old astride a white horse. He had learned so much about her it felt like he'd known her a thousand years, perhaps longer. The idea of living his life and then leaving her to live the rest of eternity alone just felt . . . cruel. He couldn't and didn't want to ever hurt her.

"I'm thinking about it, but the idea is scary as hell,"

he admitted. "I mean, there's a lot of questions I still have about it. About the very nature of life and death . . and undeath."

Her hope dimmed and she nodded, looking away. "It's scary when you're alone during the turn. In those moments when your heartbeat slows and then finally shudders to a stop, when you experience true oblivion, it's terrifying. But you wouldn't be alone. I would be there with you."

Ryan pulled her closer, his heart breaking at the thought of Grace turning into a vampire all alone in a broom closet. Cold, afraid, *dying* without knowing that it wasn't the end for her.

"I wish I had been there," he said.

Her delicate brows drew together in confusion. "Where?"

"With you, when you turned. I hate that you were abandoned the way you were." He gripped the hair at the nape of her neck, feeling the silky strands caress his skin. "What happened to him, anyway?"

"The one who sired me?"

"Yeah."

"I heard that he searched London another dozen years before leaving for America and never found his mate. He met his end at the hands of the Brotherhood of the Blood Moon."

"The brotherhood of the *what*, now?"

Grace chuckled. "I keep forgetting that you don't know anything about my world."

"Well, it's my world now too, so enlighten me." He massaged her scalp, which made her sigh in pleasure.

"The supernatural are everywhere, often hidden in plain sight. There are all sorts of societies, brotherhoods, packs, and councils in the supernatural world to keep the peace, both with humans and each other. Vampires live in covens and are governed by societies. Werewolves have councils that govern over their packs. Witches and warlocks also call their groups covens, but they are governed by the councils."

"So what happens when humans like me find out about all this? Are we forced to pick a side and become one of them?"

"Oh, humans have known about us for centuries. Humans have their own ways of keeping a balance between the others."

"Wait, is that the brotherhood you mentioned?"

Grace nodded. "The Brotherhood of the Blood Moon. Their legacy goes back more than a thousand years, and their reach spans entire continents. Their headquarters are in Detroit."

"Well, *that* I wasn't expecting. I thought it would be something classy like Rome or Oxford."

"In the past, yes, but Detroit serves their needs now. Crumbling cities often offer the best places to operate large organizations unseen."

"So they're what, the vampire, wolf, and witch police?"

"They are now. Back when I was first turned, their only goal was to exterminate us without a second thought."

"What changed?"

"The world did, and the weapons it chose to use. World War II threatened to destroy us all, and most of us took up arms to fight back the darkness. The Brotherhood saw what supernatural beings were capable of when we fought alongside them, even at our own peril, and learned that we are not all evil monsters. We are like humans—some of us are good, some bad."

"Are you saying there were also bad vampires and werewolves who fought in the war?"

"Unfortunately, yes. But there were more of us than them, and we did our best to wipe out the others. It was a show of good faith that the Brotherhood did not forget."

"You keep saying *we* . . . Did you fight too?"

Grace nodded, though a darkness fell over her face. "I served as a messenger on the front. Georgie and I worked to cross battle lines to deliver communications.

We were hard to kill, and the generals often said we had 'the devil's own luck.' If only they'd known the truth."

"So how does this all work? Is there some kind of a supernatural UN?"

"The Brotherhood meets with our councils, covens, packs, and societies. Treaties are formed, disputes handled peacefully, and rules are established for protecting humans. The Brotherhood enforces these rules, but there are those within each species who police their own kind as well. It would be unwise to have a werewolf deal with a vampire or vice versa, as it could cause tensions to rise."

Ryan pulled her a little closer, wanting to protect her. "Was that man who shot you a Brotherhood guy?"

"I doubt it. The Brotherhood are better skilled than that, and they rarely work alone. Most work in pairs, a hunter and a tracker."

"How does that work? Tracking, I mean."

"The tracker is a human who has magical abilities in their blood. They can perform spells and other enchantments to help locate supernatural creatures or fight them. They can also use their magic to protect the hunter they work with."

"So they're basically witches and warlocks?"

"After a fashion. The humans who work with the Brotherhood are not part of any coven or council. They are born into families that have belonged to the Brotherhood for centuries."

"So can you be certain it wasn't one of the Brotherhood?" he asked.

"They wouldn't go after me without a reason. And if they had, I would be dead and you would either have your memory wiped or be a guest in one of their interrogation rooms right now."

"Oh . . ." Ryan then had a new question for her. "How are you so *calm* after all that?"

"You mean the hunter?"

"Yeah. I mean, some asshole tried to kill you. I wouldn't be able to be calm about that."

She gave a weary shrug. "You get used to it. It's less scary than other things out there."

Well, that was anything but reassuring. "*What* other things?" He pulled her up a little on his body so he could see her face better.

She placed her palms on his chest, seeming more alert now.

"I had a true mate once . . . His name was William. He was a human. We hadn't fully completed our mating yet. I'd tasted his blood, but he had not shared mine. That's crucial to completing a mate's bond."

There was such sorrow in her voice, and Ryan would have given anything to take that pain and hurt away from her or share it with her so she wasn't alone.

"What happened to him?" Ryan held her as she trembled a little. It was clear that William meant something to her that he did not yet understand, but he wanted to.

She swallowed hard before continuing. "He fought in World War II and died on the fields of France. After I lost him, I became vulnerable. Gabriel saw that vulnerability and used it against me."

"Ah, right. *That* asshole," Ryan muttered.

"I didn't see the danger until it was too late. He was charming, handsome, powerful. I felt lucky to even be noticed by him. But that's how predators work. And they take that feeling and use it against you."

She was silent a long moment. He held on to her, feeling her pain as if it was his own.

"But Gabriel was worse than I could've imagined. He was no longer human. He was a warlock with real power, *dark* power. Most warlocks use white magic to help people. But Gabriel's magic had always been dark. He pretended his motivations were good, but it wasn't until I was free of him that I realized that his actions were never about *helping* someone, but *hurting* someone else."

She shivered. "To keep me with him, he cast spells

on me. *Bad* ones. Magic can't stay on a vampire forever, but his were strong enough to last a long time. Years. I moved about like a puppet, saying and doing exactly what he wanted. He would tug on a string, and I would dance. I was trapped inside my own head, trapped inside my own body. He . . ."

She closed her eyes and was so still Ryan could tell she wasn't even breathing.

"I was a living doll. I had no power, no agency of my own. He owned everything but my soul. He'd promised that loving him would take my pain away, but he never warned me it was a bargain for my free will."

A wave of rage swept through Ryan. For the first time in his life, he wanted to take a life. Take that last breath from someone's body. He wanted to kill the man who'd done this to her.

"How did you get free?" he finally asked.

"His latest spell was starting to weaken, and I was doing everything in my power to hide that knowledge from him. He sent me shopping for groceries one night, and when I got to the store, Georgie was there waiting, hiding in the produce aisle. She'd been searching for me for more than ten years. When she heard through whispers in the vampire community of someone matching my description being seen in the area, she waited in that grocery store every night for two weeks until I ran into her. I'd lost all sense of time. He'd stolen ten years from me, and I had not even been aware of it."

"I'm so sorry . . ." Ryan stroked her cheek with the backs of his fingers. "What happened once Georgie found you?"

"I'd regained enough of myself to ask for help, but she'd already pieced together most of what had happened and had a plan in place. She helped me get into a van and drove me to her coven. I warned her there was a tracker spell on me. But her coven leader, Barnabas, had mated a witch and she had cast a powerful ward over their mansion. The moment we drove through the gates, the spell was obliterated, along with the rest of his hold over me.

"For the first time in ten years, I was free, and he couldn't find me. I stayed at the coven mansion for almost a decade. When I finally did leave, the coven watched out for Gabriel to protect me. They still watch over me, which is why I'm surprised Gabriel found us at the Magic Pan. I haven't seen him in fifty years."

"He doesn't age?" Ryan asked. He knew he was only just learning about the supernatural world, but he'd thought vampires were the only ones who didn't age.

"Witches and warlocks naturally do age slower than humans, but they still have relatively the same lifespans. But when they mate with a vampire or another supernatural creature, their lifespan tends to match their supernatural mate. But Gabriel's situation is different. He isn't mated to anyone. When you dive into dark magic, there are spells for prolonging one's life, but it's a bit like that book about Dorian Gray. He looks fine on the outside, but he's decaying mentally on the inside."

"Can Gabriel be killed?" Ryan was already thinking, planning, something Jake had often teased him about. But he was already thinking about when he turned. If he was a vampire, he would be strong enough to kill this bastard for what he'd done to Grace.

"None of us are immortal, not even the dragons. But it would be a big risk."

"Wait, what? *Dragons?* There's dragons now?" He felt like he'd fallen through a rabbit hole into some *Lord of the Rings*–type dream.

Grace smiled mischievously. "We can talk all about dragons another time. I don't want to blow your little human mind."

Ryan made a mental note to bring that up later, but for now his mind raced over a hundred plans to find and kill Gabriel, only he had no idea if any of them could work. He needed to talk to Jake about what vampires were capable of. He didn't want to worry Grace with these dark thoughts.

"Can't anyone stop him? I thought you had rules."

"We could report him to the witch councils. I'm sure they'll go after him, but he's powerful and cunning. It could take them decades to find him, and even then he might talk his way out of any punishment."

They fell into silence, holding on to each other as fear for their future hung like a dark cloud above them. The sudden ringing of Ryan's phone made them both jump. He answered it when he saw his brother's name on the screen.

"Jake?"

"He's dead," Jake said. "The hunter who attacked Grace is dead."

"What? You're sure?" He sat up in bed and settled Grace on his lap. He could tell by the expression on her face that she could hear Jake talking, heightened senses and all.

"Georgie and I tracked the man from the parking lot of the Magic Pan by his scent. Even though he took a car, Georgie was still able to trail him. He went to a bar on the edge of the city, one with a fairly bad reputation. When we got there, cops were all over the place. He was hit by a car crossing the street. The police were taking photos and collecting evidence. He's gone."

There was a moment of pure relief, and Ryan's grip

around Grace tightened a little. He wanted to hug her and never let her go. It was then, when the danger was over, that he realized just what Grace had come to mean to him in so short a time. She was . . . everything. He'd never known he could feel that way about someone, not after how things had ended with Mandy. Yet here his heart was beating out a rhythm that spelled her name over and over.

"So Grace is safe," Ryan concluded after a moment's silence.

"Yes." Jake's voice was full of relief. "You guys can go home and get on with, well, *things*."

Ryan grinned. His brother was fishing for information about how things were going with him and Grace. Soon Jake would hear the good news, that *things* with Grace were going well, so well that he was set on being her mate, whenever she decided to ask him.

"I'll take Grace home so she can get some fresh clothes, and then we'll get on with those *things*." He used the same vague wording just to tease his brother.

"What about you and me? Are we good?" Jake sounded so worried that Ryan felt his own heart twinge.

"More or less. But we're still due for a long talk, you and I."

"You got it." Jake's voice relaxed. "I'm glad you

know the truth. I hated keeping it from you, but you have to admit, there was no easy way to break it to you."

"I know." Ryan's gaze drifted to Grace as she leaned in and kissed his cheek. The kiss was meant to comfort him, and it did. Grace was no brooding Gothic vampire set on the seduction of mortal men for their blood. She was simply Grace, sweet, sexy, smart Grace. Sure, she had fangs, but what relationship didn't have its challenges? He couldn't even imagine his life without her now.

"We'll talk soon?" Jake asked.

"Sure thing." Ryan hung up and turned to Grace. She gazed at him with a focused intensity, but he liked it, and he knew he watched her in the same way. It was like he was a teenager with a crush all over again. He'd forgotten what it felt like to desire someone so much that he felt more than a little crazy.

He shifted her closer on his lap, very aware of how she intimately straddled him.

"So . . . ," she began.

"So . . . ," he echoed with his best lazy grin.

Grace inched closer, their bodies creating a delicious friction. She cupped his face in her palms and her mouth sought his, claiming him in a way that both unmade him and put him back together. He wrapped his arms around her, holding her tight. She moaned against his lips as though his possessive hold made her burn all that much hotter.

"What . . . what are we going to do about us?" he murmured against her lips. "Because I want to *keep* you, keep you forever, and I don't even know what that means. I only know it's true."

He fisted a hand in her hair and held her head still for his ravenous kisses. Grace met him kiss for kiss as if they had been starved for each other for centuries.

"Then keep me," she whispered. "Be my mate, Ryan."

They rested their foreheads against each other and shared a breath.

"Yes," he said, and the single word had a promise of forever.

Her lashes flew up. "Yes?" She stared at him in a state of wonder.

"Yes. You jump, I jump," he vowed. He'd never meant anything more in his life. He would do anything for this woman. He'd only just met her, but feeling this true mate thing had given him an amazing sense of clarity about what he wanted in life. And he wanted her.

The smile on her face shone brighter than the sun, and the warmth of it burned clear through to his very soul. He would never be cold again, not when his woman, *his mate*, smiled at him like that.

"Let me prove it to you," he growled playfully and toppled her back down on the bed. She fell beneath him, and her giggles turned to gasps as he showed her just how happy he was that he had gone on that blind date with a vampire.

GRACE AND RYAN STAYED AT THE MOTEL THE REST OF THE DAY, making love even though the sunlight made her sleepy. She rather liked the slow claiming of her body as she lay relaxed and drowsy beneath him. He didn't seem to tire, and neither did she. They existed in their own world. But when night fell, they knew it was time to leave.

"So we'll go back to your place," Ryan said as he lifted one booted foot onto the edge of a chair by the window so he could tie his laces. They'd already agreed that it would be a good idea for Grace to lie low in case Gabriel decided to make another unexpected appearance. In the meantime, Georgie was going to her coven and the Salem Witch Council to seek their help in finding Gabriel.

"And I'll pack up my work stuff and a week's worth of clothes," she continued.

"Right." He tied his other boot, then retrieved his car keys, wallet, and phone from the bedside table.

After a long and adventurous day in bed together, she'd told him she wanted to stay at his place for a while rather than at her coven's mansion, to see how living together felt. It probably felt fast for mortals, but it would be hard for her to be away from him for too long. The deeper their bond became, the harder it was to resist her need for him. Rather than be disturbed by that, Ryan seemed comfortable with her intruding on his personal space so soon. The thought of his ready acceptance of her made her strangely giddy. She'd told him everything she knew about vampire mates and what it meant to be bonded, and it hadn't scared him away.

It was an hour after sundown when they reached her apartment. She retrieved her keys from her purse, and they headed up the stairs to the second floor. She unlocked her door and caught the scent of danger a second too late. Pain crippled her, and she fell to her knees, gasping for breath.

She'd been hit with a spell, one she was all too familiar with. Gabriel had used this spell in the past to prevent her from escaping or from attacking him.

"Grace!" Ryan caught her in his arms and crouched beside her. "What's wrong?"

"R-run," she gasped. "*Run!*"

Gabriel's cold voice echoed from inside her apartment. "Oh, I'm afraid it's far too late for that."

She raised her face to the door as it opened the rest of the way. Gabriel was standing there, a grim look darkening his handsome face into a look of absolute cruelty.

"*Far* too late, Grace," he said again. The warlock raised his palm. His dark magic swirled in a ball of dangerous red energy. She knew that spell, and if it hit a human, it would be fatal.

Gabriel aimed his palm at Ryan.

"No!" She shoved Ryan out of the way, and the blast hit Grace in the chest. Pain like she'd never felt in her life except when William had died consumed her.

"You fool!" Gabriel snarled. "That wasn't meant for you!"

Grace collapsed on the floor, gasping out of instinct rather than need. Odd thoughts formed, and her mind began to stray as her body struggled not to die for a second time. Was she truly going to die this time? Was it possible? And Ryan . . . She couldn't protect him, not if she died . . .

She thought she heard Ryan's shouts of rage and

objects crashing all around her. She blinked slowly as she tried to see what was happening. Gabriel and Ryan were fighting in the middle of the room, and Ryan was . . . *winning*? How was that possible?

The two men were squared off. Ryan held a knife, and they clashed together again in a brawl, but then moments later, a blinding red light flashed in the room and Ryan was flung away from Gabriel. The power of whatever spell had been cast momentarily stunned Grace's senses. Her ears rang with a cacophony of sounds from miles away that normally she could repress, and her vision was streaked with a flash of brilliant colors that made her head throb.

Slowly, she began to recover, her vampire essence restoring her strength. Furniture was overturned, lamps were broken, books scattered on the floor. Her life was being destroyed, but that didn't matter. Only one thing mattered now.

Her mate.

In the time it took her to stand, the tide had turned against Ryan. He now lay on his back in the middle of the floor, unmoving. Gabriel was propped against a nearby wall, blood dripping down his face. He held a hand to his chest where a large kitchen knife protruded.

Gabriel must have used most if not all of his magic in that blast. It had left him weakened, vulnerable, *mortal.* His hand shook, covered in blood, as he removed the blade. He cried out, unaccustomed to feeling such pain, only inflicting it.

Grace crawled to her mate, still hearing the faint beat of his heart. "Ryan . . ."

"Your mortal is doomed." Gabriel's voice was full of acid. "Damned fool thought he could fight a warlock. Guess he did." Gabriel let the knife fall to the floor, and Grace heard his heartbeat turning erratic. Gabriel was dying.

"What did you do to him?" Grace demanded. Her body was still fighting against the blast of magic Gabriel had hit her with, but her strength was returning.

Gabriel smiled, blood coating his teeth as he coughed.

"A blood curse, my dear. Took the last of my magic to do it . . ." He coughed again, more weakly this time, and fell to his knees. "I did it . . . for you. For us."

For you. Grace wanted to spit in Gabriel's face and call out his sentiments for the lies they were.

"You never listened," he said. "We were always meant to . . . be together. I only wanted to . . . save you from your pain."

"You never understood," she whispered. "Love is pain, love is joy. When you lose someone you love and it hurts so much that you feel like you're dying . . . you know it's real. I never wanted to be saved from the pain of losing William. I wanted someone to love to ease it, to find my way back to joy."

Their eyes locked for a moment, and she saw confusion clouding Gabriel's eyes. He still didn't understand what it meant to love someone. Now he never would, and she . . . she was losing Ryan.

"Tell me how to reverse it." Grace bared her fangs and faced him. Her fingers curled into claws and her voice deepened.

Something changed in Gabriel's eyes, and for the first time she saw he *feared* her. Finally. But it was too late . . . far too late for all of them.

"There is a way to stop it . . . but it comes with a price."

Grace's heart turned cold with fear and dread. All dark magic came with a terrible price.

"How do I save him? What must I do?"

The warlock's eyes were losing their light bit by bit, and she knew she was losing precious time to save her mate.

"One kiss from you and the poison vanishes from his blood. But the curse will stay. He'll lose all memory of you and will never be able to remember you ever again. He will live, but he will be lost to you forever. A mate you can never claim, never turn."

"No . . ." Grace stared at Gabriel in horror. "Undo it, you must—"

"Once it's cast, a blood curse cannot be reversed. It was . . . the only way forward." Gabriel reached for her, hoping for one last reassuring touch. "Only . . . way . . ." He sighed and his arm fell to his side. The erratic pulse of his heart, once as dark as his magic, ceased.

"Grace?" Ryan breathed, the sound full of pain.

"I'm here," she called back to him, cradling his head in her lap. His brown eyes fixed on hers.

"I heard . . . cursed me . . ."

"Yes, but I can undo it," she promised and stroked his hair, fighting back tears. "It's okay. I can save you."

He tried to shake his head and lifted one hand to catch her wrist. "I heard . . . I won't remember you. I don't want that . . . I want to keep you. Want to love you . . . for a thousand years." Ryan's voice broke with pain and emotion.

"There's no other way." Grace tried to keep her voice steady, but failed.

"There has to be . . . I won't let them take you from me. I'll call Georgie and Jake. We'll think of something . . . We . . ." His heartbeat stuttered dangerously, and he shuddered in her arms.

"I'm sorry. I'm so sorry. I wish we had more time," she whispered, her eyes burning with tears. "But in the moments I was with you . . . you were mine. I'll always be there, watching over you. Promise me that you'll have an exquisite life. Every sunrise you see, every wave that crashes onto the shores, that will be me, kissing you or whispering your name."

"No," he said firmly, tears in his eyes as he used the last bit of his strength as he held on to her wrist. That was the thing about humans—they had such a strength inside them, something that drove them beyond the limits of creatures stronger than them. Love was a force that gave nearly endless strength to those who bathed in its glow.

"I'll watch over you," she promised. "Even though you won't remember."

"Find a way. *Make* me remember you. *Don't let me go.*"

The desperation in his voice would haunt her for as long as she lived. But he didn't understand. Some things could not be undone. She had only one choice. To save him, she had to lose him.

She bent her head to his. The moment her lips touched his, she felt the darkness of the blood curse inside Ryan. She drew it into herself, allowing the dark energy to battle her potent vampire blood, knowing the vampire in her would triumph.

Ryan's eyes cleared of pain, and an instant later, she saw his love for her and all his memories fade into a cloudy confusion before he slipped into unconsciousness, but his heartbeat was strong and healthy. But hers . . . hers shattered like the finest porcelain on stone, becoming nothing more than slender shards and dust.

Grace held him, stroking his hair from his face. She wiped away tears and realized that her fangs had nicked her lip when she'd been hit by the spell. As she wiped at her eyes, a drop of her blood fell from her lips onto his mouth. She drew in a shuddering breath, glad for once that she wasn't human. Her heart never would have survived what it was enduring right now. She had lost a mate for a second time . . . but at least he would have a wonderful life, a *mortal* life. It was all she could give him, and it would have to be enough.

"I love you. I'll love you until I'm nothing more than cosmic dust," she vowed.

Her beautiful mate slept on, unaware of his memories of her fading away.

EIGHT

Three months later

Thunder crashed, and Ryan bolted upright in his bed. His apartment was pitch-black except for the occasional flash of lightning coming through the windows. He fought to catch his breath and calm his racing heart.

Fragments of a dream clung to his skin, caressing him with invisible hands. An intoxicating scent lingered in the air. He breathed deep, but already the scent was fading and the feel of a woman in his arms was slipping away. She was gone. That nameless specter that haunted his dreams was gone again. He could conjure no face, no memory, only a bone-deep sense that something that meant the world to him, something *priceless*, was gone.

He'd had this dream so often, especially when it rained. Each time he woke, a ghost of memory lingered about him, breaking him further. He felt like a stone slowly fracturing with an unseen pressure crushing in on him from all sides. These dreams . . . they were battering the walls of reality, demanding entry to his sanity. He wasn't sure how much more he could take.

Ryan kicked the covers away and got out of bed. It was close to midnight now. A storm raged on the horizon outside his window, and another burst of light illuminated the dark world outside.

Was that a figure on the street below? A moment later, a second lightning strike flashed. The figure was gone. He pressed a palm flat upon the glass and continued to watch the spot for a long while. Had he imagined that feminine figure in the dark?

Too restless to sleep, he finally dressed and grabbed his keys. He needed a drink, and he didn't want to do that alone in his apartment. He drove to a bar that he and Jake liked to visit on Friday nights when they had brother time, just the two of them. It was a popular little place called the Atlas Pub. It was busy most of the time, but tonight's storm and the late hour had driven away most of the customers.

Ryan took a seat at the bar, and the bartender, recognizing him, poured him a whiskey. There were only a dozen people here, most of whom were quietly drinking away their sorrows, just like he was. Drinking for a sorrow he couldn't even place.

"Slow night," Ryan observed.

"Rain always keeps the crowds down," the bartender said before another customer waved him down for a drink.

Ryan held the glass between his palms, rolling it over and over as he watched the liquid swirl in the glass. The remnants of the dream still clung to him, and yet he couldn't remember much other than that he felt *lost*.

Someone sat down beside him, and he glanced to his right, seeing a woman with long blonde hair. She smiled tentatively at him. He tried to focus on her face, but it was strangely hard to do so.

"Hi," she said after a moment.

"Hi," he replied, a bit baffled. Most women did not start conversations with strange men in a bar, especially this time of night.

Suddenly his mind blanked, and he found himself alone. Had he been alone this whole time? He thought he remembered talking to someone.

He glanced around at the rest of the bar and then back down at his drink, sighing heavily.

He was supposed to remember something . . . but

what? That deep nagging feeling never left him. If anything, it had gotten stronger.

"Bar's closing. You need coffee for the road?" the bartender asked.

Ryan stared at his empty glass of whiskey. He'd gotten here before 1:00 a.m., and the bar closed at 3:00. He checked the clock on the wall and blinked. It was 2:50 a.m. How had he lost track of time?

"No, thanks. I'm good." Ryan settled his tab, then headed for his car. He'd had only one glass of whiskey, and that had been two hours ago, and he didn't even remember drinking it. He wasn't drunk, not even close, so he knew he was safe to drive, but he'd clearly zoned out while he was in the pub, and that wasn't good.

He stared at the car and wiped the rain from his eyes. Why had he come here? He barely remembered even waking up and getting here. He pulled out his cell phone and called his brother.

"Jake?"

"You okay, little bro?" Jake didn't sound tired. Maybe he couldn't sleep either.

"I did it again . . . I don't remember why I left my apartment."

"Where are you?"

"The Atlas Pub."

"I'll be there in ten minutes. Wait for me in your car."

"Okay." Ryan hung up and got in the driver's seat. He felt like an idiot for calling on his older brother like this. He felt like a child again, lost and needing his big brother's help all the time.

Rain tapped on the windows. He closed his eyes, searching that vast hollowness inside him that offered no explanation. He imagined diving into that dark, endless abyss. The moment he did, he felt it, that ghostly presence of something. A memory of a memory. Rain . . . a car . . . feminine hands in his, her lips caressing his . . . That was all he could ever find in the endless darkness. His heart clenched so tight he could barely breathe. The grief of losing what he could not remember was killing him.

"Ryan?"

He jolted out of that darkness at the sound of his brother tapping on the window.

"Y-yeah," he choked out as he rolled the window down. Jake bent down and rested his elbows on the car's open windowsill.

"You okay?"

"What do you think?" Ryan said quietly and scrubbed a hand along his jaw, feeling three days' worth of growth there scratching his palm. "What the hell is wrong with me, Jake? Am I losing my mind?"

Jake tried to smile, but it was forced. "You aren't losing your mind."

"Then you explain this."

His brother's brows knitted together. "I can't. Maybe you're overworked?"

Overwork never felt like this, though. "It's like something is lost. And I can't find it." He choked down the words that were too painful to say. *I can't find my way home. Only home's not a place, it's someone, but I don't know who.*

"Let me drive you, okay?"

Ryan slid to the passenger side and let Jake take him home, but it wasn't really *home*. He felt like he never would be home again.

GRACE SAT ON THE BARSTOOL AT THE ATLAS PUB AND STARED at her glass of water.

"You okay, honey?" the bartender asked her. He was a middle-aged man with gray threading his hair at the temples. He seemed tough, but there was a gentleness in his eyes that betrayed him by revealing his innate kindness.

She drew in a deep breath, inhaling the intoxicating masculine scent that Ryan had left behind.

"I'm all right," she lied.

She'd been *right there* beside him. So close she could reach out and touch him. But she hadn't dared to. The last time she'd done that she'd lost him that much sooner. That was the part that drove a stake through her heart. Seeing his expression fade and go blank and his eyes turn distant as all memory of her was erased once again . . . It was enough to shatter her heart.

Tonight she'd spoken to him. She knew she shouldn't. Knew it was pointless. That it would only hurt them both. But for one beautiful instant he'd *seen* her before she'd lost him to the curse once again.

She'd sat with Ryan, unable to bear leaving him as he gazed into his glass of whiskey, unmoving, unseeing. Then, finally, she'd left. She had to let him go, even though she knew at some point she'd be right there beside him again. Hoping.

She'd stood in the rain and shadows, watched him call his brother to come get him. Then she went back into the bar and took her seat again.

"I don't know what's wrong with that fellow," the bartender said. "You talk to him every time he's here, and he just goes dark on you. I don't get it. You seem sweet. His head must be full of rocks, that one," the bartender muttered. "Well, it's closing time. You drive safe, honey, all right?"

"I will. Thank you." Grace left the pub and faced the rain-soaked predawn morning. Later as she lay in bed, the pale light of a perfect spring morning tiptoed into her bedroom through the mostly closed blinds. While the birds chattered outside, completely content with the world, Grace let out a shuddering sound somewhere between a sob and a cry of pain. Life kept moving on around her. She was forever left behind . . . in the dark, stormy shadows.

"We have to do something, Georgie," Jake said as he took his love into his arms. "I'm worried we're losing him." Jake tried to keep the emotion out of his voice, but Georgie must have heard his pain and desperation because she pressed herself closer against him.

"I know." She nuzzled his chest and wrapped her arms around his waist. "I was thinking I should call my friend Tamsin Batsford. She just flew in from

London to visit the Salem Witch Council in Boston. She's one of the most powerful witches of her generation. If anyone can find a way to counter Gabriel's spell, it's her."

Jake was too afraid to cling to that hope. He had watched his brother suffer for three months now. The blood curse had erased every memory associated with Grace from the moment they met. That meant Jake was back where he started with his brother, who no longer remembered vampires even existed, and they couldn't talk about anything. That invisible wall was back up between them.

Ryan seemed okay when he was busy with work, but when he got home, he spiraled out. Especially when it rained. Jake was afraid Ryan might become an even worse workaholic in order to avoid what he was feeling.

On the really bad days, Ryan would end up somewhere in the city well after midnight, not remembering how he had gotten there. He was searching for Grace, even if he didn't know it. But no matter how many times he was told about her, he could not remember anything of the past, and seeing her would erase his memory all over again.

It was destroying him from the inside out, and Jake feared at some point Ryan would break apart and it would be impossible to put him back together.

"What if we turn him? Magic doesn't stay long on a vampire, right? Wouldn't that break the spell?"

Georgie shook her head and wrapped her arms tighter around him. "I already asked about that. Tamsin said blood curses like Gabriel's evolve. Even if he turned into a vampire, the curse of the memory loss would stay."

Georgie was quiet a long moment. "She said because blood curses evolve, sometimes you can change the course of the curse's evolution. She wants to meet Ryan tomorrow and examine him for herself. She'll get a better sense of the curse if she is close enough to him. I thought we might have him over tomorrow for the party and she could meet him then."

"Okay," Jake agreed. "How's Grace? Have you spoken to her recently?"

"A few times," Georgie said. "She knows she shouldn't meet with Ryan, but sometimes she can't help it. Each time she hopes it will be different, and then..."

"And then I get a call from him and he doesn't know where he is or why he's left his apartment. She has to stop doing that, for both of their sakes."

"I know. She knows. But she can't help it. She's hurting as much as Ryan is. You know how it feels to miss your mate. You know what it's like . . ." Georgie's voice broke on a little sob. "It's not fair. That bastard did this to her, and then he died and she's still in agony."

"We'll find a way. We have to," Jake said. He wasn't going to let his brother, or Grace, fade into despair. "Make the call."

THE FOLLOWING NIGHT, JAKE WATCHED RYAN ACROSS THE crowded room at his apartment as Ryan spoke to a pretty female vampire who was flirting with him. Of course, Ryan had no idea the woman was a vampire.

"She's here," Georgie whispered excitedly as she crept up next to Jake. The party was in full swing, a celebration for Barnabas and his witchy mate. Poor Ryan was the only human, and thankfully he had no idea that he was walking among vampires, shifters, and witchfolk.

The crowd parted as a young woman with golden hair flowing down her shoulders walked through the front door. Power radiated from her like the soft shine of some ancient star. She truly shimmered, at least in the eyes of supernatural people like him. Jake was sure Ryan wouldn't see her magic the way he did.

Tamsin Batsford's features were pretty, like a girl next door, yet her smile seemed to intensify the overall effect of her presence. More than one unmated male vampire leaned close to take in Tamsin's scent in hopes of recognizing a true mate.

"That's Tamsin?"

Georgie nodded. "She's the seventh child of the seventh child from an already powerful bloodline. She has more power in her than you'll ever see again in any witch, I promise you. Great things will come once her full power is awakened."

Jake sized up the witch. "All that matters to me is if she can help Ryan or not."

"Only one way to find out." Georgie escorted him to the witch and made the introductions.

The moment Tamsin took his hand in hers, Jake felt power tingling all the way up his arm, and he had to admit, it was a bit unnerving. He felt as if she could ignite that power on a whim and reduce him to ash if she wanted.

"It's nice to meet you, Jake," she said in a soft voice. Her eyes were gentle, as though she'd grown up living amid old libraries and secret gardens. There was something so mysterious about her. It reminded him of how no matter how much he learned about Georgie, there were always more secrets to learn. It was one of the joys of finding a mate—that endless journey of learning and loving.

"Thank you for coming." Jake cleared his throat and gave a nod in Ryan's direction. "That's my brother over there."

"The one with the blood curse? I admit, the details Georgie provided me of this matter intrigued me. I should go speak with him." She walked toward Ryan, and everyone else in the room gave her space. She spoke softly to Ryan, then took his hand in hers and held it for a long moment before she reached up and touched his cheek in a motherly way before stepping back and then returning to Jake and Georgie. Ryan stood there in a daze, then shook it off and looked around, puzzled.

"It is perhaps the most powerful blood curse I've ever encountered. I'm no longer surprised that Gabriel died in his fight with your brother. He must have sunk every last drop of power and malice he had into it."

That sounded bad. "Is there any hope?" Jake asked.

"There's *always* hope," Tamsin said. "White magic is stronger than dark magic and always will be. White magic draws its power from love, and there's no stronger love than a true mate's love. Unfortunately, breaking the chains forged by dark magic can be a lethal experience. However . . ." Tamsin paused, thoughtful. "Georgie, I thought you said he hadn't taken her blood, but I saw evidence that he *does* have vampire blood in him. No more than a drop, but it's there inside him."

"Is that bad?" Georgie asked in a low voice.

Tamsin shook her head. "Perhaps not, but I think it is what is making him so miserable. That drop is a bond to Grace, reminding him that he is missing something. You said he goes out at night, searching for his mate. That single drop of blood is fighting against the blood curse Gabriel put on him, but it is not enough to break it. Nor is the curse able to subdue Grace's blood because she is Ryan's mate. But he needs more of Grace's blood, repeated exposure to his mate and her blood. It may take years, but I believe the blood curse can be overcome."

"What about his memories?" Jake asked.

"With any luck, one day, the barriers the spell created will fade and the love inside her blood will make him remember and break the chains the blood curse has him wrapped in."

"We need to call Grace." Georgie reached for her phone.

"Yes," Tamsin agreed. "You must reach her now

before it's too late. She's leaving . . . I saw it when I touched Ryan's hand. I get visions sometimes about other people's mates."

"Leaving?" Georgie gasped and shared a horrified look with Jake.

"We have to stop her," Tamsin said. "If you want to save Ryan, we can't let her leave town. The further she gets from him, the harder it will be to defeat the blood curse."

"Then let's go, Tamsin. You can get me there in time, right?" Georgie held out a hand to her friend, and Tamsin grinned.

"You bet I can."

GRACE STARED AT THE APARTMENT SHE HAD LIVED IN FOR THE last ten years. It was time to say goodbye, time to move on. She had been here too long anyway. At a certain point, people would start to notice she didn't age. Even though she lived in Cauldron Falls, her landlord was human and was one of the few residents of the city who didn't realize that Cauldron Falls was populated by supernatural creatures.

The town's human reputation was that of a Halloween-obsessed city, but in truth it was a sanctuary for creatures like her. Still, change was good, and that meant leaving all of this behind. She would return to England. Perhaps living in London would dull the sting of the endlessly empty future she faced without Ryan.

"Grace?" Georgie's voice intruded on her thoughts.

She spun around. Her friend stood there in the dark parking lot, hands in her coat pockets, and beside her was a woman Grace didn't recognize. There was no sign of another car, and she hadn't heard anyone approach on foot.

"How did you—"

The woman beside Georgie held up a hand, and gold light blossomed like a rose in her palm. A witch.

"Grace, this is Tamsin. She brought me here before it was too late."

"Too late for what?" Grace asked.

"To stop you from leaving." Georgie waved at Grace's car, which was packed full of her belongings.

Grace didn't want to leave her friend, but staying here was too painful. "I have to. Staying here is *killing* me."

Her friend's eyes softened. "I know. But you trust me, don't you?"

A lump formed in Grace's throat. "Of course I do." Georgie had always been there for her. She'd saved Grace when she'd first been turned, and again from Gabriel all those years ago, risking her own life to do it.

"How strong are you, Grace?" The witch's voice was soft and musical and full of white magic.

"What do you mean?"

"There may be a way to outlast the blood curse, but it will not be easy. You can still save your mate, and yourself."

"Save Ryan?" She flinched at the pain saying his name caused deep in her soul.

The witch walked toward her, magic shimmering around her like a veiled nebula shot through with starlight. She took Grace's hands in her own, and the warmth in her body flowed into Grace.

"Before you kissed him, a single drop of your blood entered Ryan's body, and it has been fighting the curse every moment since, but it's not enough. Imagine what sharing more of your blood will do? Your love is in every drop of blood you give him. It's that love that defies and beats back the dark magic of the blood curse." Tamsin squeezed her hands gently.

Grace stared into Tamsin's eyes as she explained that it could be *years* before her mate was saved.

"So I ask you again, how strong are you, Grace? How long can you fight for him?"

"Now that I have hope? I can fight for him forever."

"Good. Then here is what you must do . . ."

Grace listened, and for the first time in months, she no longer felt like she was drowning. She could see the shore, and it was so close now. So very close.

What were years to a vampire when they had hope of being with their true mate?

RYAN DREAMED AGAIN OF THAT NAMELESS, FACELESS PRESENCE that brought him the most peaceful joy he had ever known, only to feel it's painful absence every time he woke.

He tossed fitfully and lay on his back, listening to the rain outside. Ghostly lips touched his and he tasted something foreign upon his tongue before he lost himself in the dream that magical kiss created. When the ghostly kiss ended, he lay still, his body weary, as though he had struggled in a mighty battle and could at last rest.

For the first time he dreamed of something new, a

flash of deep blue eyes, eyes that held more mysteries than the sea, eyes that looked upon him with a love that stretched out forever. He wanted to give those eyes a name, to call for them and hold on to the peace and love that gazing into those eyes gave him.

When he drifted back to sleep, his lips formed a name.

"Grace..."

CHAPTER

NINE

Valentine's Day—Two years later

Ryan checked his watch as he sat in the bar of a restaurant called the Magic Pan. Had he really agreed to go on a blind date? Jake had talked him into it, and he was not looking forward to the inevitable awkward encounter of meeting a random stranger.

Jake was right, he was getting older. It was time he settled down. The last two years he'd been restless, searching, drifting, trying to find a piece of himself that was missing. He wanted to be in love, he wanted to get married and share his life with someone.

But a blind date? What had he been thinking? These things never went well.

The bar seats beside him opened up a little as a

couple left, carrying their drinks to a table. Without warning, a wild rush of excitement swept through Ryan and he turned, not sure what he was expecting to see.

A woman had taken one of the empty seats, her blonde hair tumbling in loose waves about her shoulders. She wore a black skirt and a deep blue blouse that matched the stunning shade of her eyes.

Those eyes . . . An electric volt shot through his heart. It felt like he was pounding on the closed door inside his head.

Remember, a voice urged. *Remember . . .*

Remember what?

"Hi," the woman said, her smile warmer than the sun.

"Hi," he replied, but he felt like an idiot. That had sounded so lame. What happened to the charmer he used to be?

"You're Ryan, right?" the woman asked with a soft smile that was sweeter, more intimate somehow, as if she knew a secret and was sharing it with him.

"Um, yeah. Wait, are you . . . ?" He reached for his phone to check the name his brother had texted him.

"Grace." She held out her hand. "I'm Grace."

Ryan grinned back at her bashfully and shook her hand. The moment their palms connected, he felt a surge of *knowing*. That was the only way he could describe it. Somehow he *knew* this woman. Like he'd spent a thousand lifetimes dreaming of her face and breathing her name in the dark.

Grace.

"I'm sorry, but . . . have we met before?" He leaned in a little, wanting to be closer to her. "Maybe at one of Jacob and Georgie's parties?"

Grace gazed up at him with those eyes as deep as the sea and cupped his face with one hand.

She nibbled her bottom lip and closed the distance between them. Their lips met. Sweet fire burst forth from that kiss, and his head throbbed as a thousand visions . . . no . . . *memories* . . . cascaded through him in a waterfall of colors, sounds, and sensations.

Grace here at the bar but a different night. Grace with an arrow in her belly. Him cradling her in his arms as she revealed what she really was. Kissing her in bed, the passion between them like twin souls finding one another. Grace soaked from the rain and crying in her car. Grace in a hotel shower with him. Grace kissing him one last time as he lay dying. Phantom kisses in the dark, murmurs of love.

"Remember me . . . please remember."

"Hold on to me, Ryan. Just a little longer. Each night, we have a little more time. Keep fighting with me."

"Grace—Grace? What's happening to me?" Ryan

was overwhelmed with everything he was feeling and remembering. A tide of grief and longing swept through him so harshly that it threatened to drown him. "I remember . . . I remember everything . . ."

"Shh, it's okay," Grace soothed and kissed him again. "It's okay. I love you . . . I *love* you, Ryan. I will do this for a hundred years if I have to."

"Do what?" He cupped the back of her neck and pressed his forehead to hers, holding on as he feared she would vanish.

"I will kiss you and make you remember me. Every time you hold on to the memory of me just a little bit longer." She smiled, and her eyes glittered with tears. "I won't give up on us. Focus on the night we first met at the Magic Pan. Do you remember?"

Ryan nodded. "I remember feeling like an idiot for meeting you in the bar and not knowing you were my date and how damned happy I was when I figured out it was you." He cupped her face in his hands, studying her, so afraid he'd forget. "What happened . . . after Gabriel . . . ?"

"You couldn't remember . . . and I kept coming to you, but it made it worse, until a witch told me you needed more of my blood to fight the curse. I've been coming to you every night, fighting for you, for us."

"And I . . ." He forgot what he was about to say,

forgot what they were even speaking about. Suddenly, it was hard to focus, hard to even think.

He could already feel her slipping away, the memories first, then her name, and last her face. It was like a black night closing in around him. He wasn't going to let it happen again. He wasn't going to lose the love of his life.

Some deep, primal voice inside him roared in rage and defiance. Not this time. Not again. *Not again.*

This time it would be different. It had to be. The wall began to thin, the memories, her face, her name becoming clear once again.

"Grace … Grace …"

"Ryan?" Grace whispered, her voice full of pain and hope.

"I'm not letting go of you, not this time." His body shook as he felt the last vestiges of the curse trying to take over, the invisible chains tightening around his mind, but he loved Grace too much to let it win. Those chains began to crack, then break . . . and finally fall away. He could breathe again.

He relaxed and closed his eyes. The memories didn't fade. He blinked slowly, feeling like he was stepping into bright sunlight after a lifetime in a cave.

"How long … ? How long have we … ?" He couldn't

finish. The pain of feeling all the time they had lost was like a knife in his heart.

"Two years."

"Two *years*?" He pulled her closer until she slid off the barstool, and he simply held her in his arms. She smelled of jasmine and lavender. God, he had missed that scent.

"Two years," she echoed. Now she was the one shaking.

He remembered it all now. Every night of loneliness, and Grace . . . slipping into his bed, kissing him, giving him a hint of her blood, bonding him to her so that this day would someday come.

Grace buried her face against his chest and wept. He kissed the crown of her hair and then her forehead, and finally he made her tilt her face back so he could kiss her again.

"I love you," he whispered. "I loved you before I even knew you. You are my dawn and my dusk, all the twilight that lies between." He kissed her deeply and she sighed softly, melting in his arms.

"You're mine forever," he told her. "My vampire valentine."

She laughed in weepy delight at that, and the sound of it was like joyous church bells ringing on a clear winter morning. He now understood what his brother had wanted for him all along. He'd wanted Ryan to know this joy, this endless love.

"We'd better call Jake and Georgie so we can make some preparations," he said, thinking now of their future and what it would mean.

"For what?" she asked uncertainly.

"For my turning," he whispered in her ear. "I don't want to waste another minute. Let's go home. I've missed you more than you can ever know. I have two years of making love to you to catch up on."

"If a vampire could blush, I would be," she replied with a giggle.

They left the restaurant and walked toward his car, hand in hand.

"I'm a lucky man," he said as they stopped beneath the bright moonlight.

She gazed up at him, her hands tucked in his.

"Two years . . . So I've had hundreds of chances to meet you and fall in love with you for the first time."

Grace smiled but then turned solemn. "We've lost so much time . . ."

"Anything in this world worth having, *anyone* worth loving, is worth fighting for. And I'd fight to love you for a thousand more years, *vampire mine.*"

He tipped her chin and leaned down to steal another kiss as his beloved swooned in his arms. He feathered his lips over hers, savoring that faint kiss before he deepened it.

"Vampire mine," she echoed. "I like that."

Ryan smiled when he felt her lips curve up in an echoing grin. He'd been blind for so long, but now he could see. The universe he held in his arms was simply stunning . . . simply *everything*.

TURN THE PAGE TO READ THE FIRST CHAPTER OF *THE BITE of Winter*, **where a young woman down on her luck falls hard for two Irish bachelor vampires.**

THE BITE OF WINTER

So hungry. God, I'd kill to eat.

Zoey Blake gazed longingly through the diner window. Families were nestled in red leather booths, plates of burgers and fries spread out like a feast. The light from the diner beckoned to her, promising warmth and comfort. It was everything she wanted, and everything she couldn't have.

The harsh December wind cut through her thin flannel shirt and whipped her hair hard enough to sting her face. Hunger swelled up inside her like an empty balloon. A moan escaped her lips as she tried and failed to ignore the pain.

A little boy in one of the booths reached with chubby hands to grab his mother's milkshake. He sucked for a long moment on the straw before pulling back, a grin of delight on his face. Zoey could imagine the thick creamy ice cream and the sweet tangy taste of a maraschino cherry.

One of the cooks left the grill and walked toward the entrance, wiping his hands on his greasy apron. When the door swung open, Christmas music exploded into the street. The happy sounds reminded Zoey that Christmas was only a few weeks away. She used to love Christmas: the songs, the presents, the food...her family. She shuddered and buried the painful memories deep inside her.

The cook glanced down the empty street outside the diner and caught sight of her.

"You coming in?" His gruff voice momentarily distracted her from the greasy smell of food.

Zoey gulped and took an instinctive step back, her hands clutching the only real possession she had left in the world. A black leather portfolio. She'd tucked it safely against her chest, the leather barely holding warmth to her body.

"Sorry, I...I can't..." She couldn't say the words. *Can't afford it.*

Even after a year of living on the streets, shame still heated her cheeks. This time, she welcomed it. She was cold all the time, even in the summer. Her jacket had been stolen the winter before, leaving her painfully exposed.

The cook's eyes hardened.

"Then get going. You're scaring off paying customers."

Of course she had to leave. Heaven forbid he toss her some of the burnt burgers or even some moldy buns. She'd have gladly taken them. Far worse food had ended up in her stomach when she'd been desperate.

With a shaky nod, Zoey backed away from the diner and eased into the shadows where the restaurant's light couldn't penetrate. She just wanted to disappear. No one would miss her. No one would care. Everyone she had a connection with was gone. And it was all her fault.

Unshed tears formed at the corners of her eyes, and a shiver from the cold rattled her spine so hard it hurt. Self-pity was not something she could indulge in. But it was hard to ignore her circumstances when she'd spent the last month calling a ragged sleeping bag under a highway overpass home. Food was harder to come by than a decent place to sleep. The homeless shelter was half a mile away and always filled up so fast they had to turn away most of the people who showed up. They served only two meals a day with small portions since their food bank supplies remained low.

Her stomach rumbled a protest. She had to stop thinking about food.

"Damn it." She put her fist in her mouth, stumbling back into the alleyway next to the diner. The ache inside bent her over, and she wrapped her arms around her waist, hugging herself as she prayed the pain would begin to dull. Finally, it abated, briefly, and she leaned back against the brick wall of the alley, breathing slowly.

A soft scuffling was her only warning.

Zoey's eyes flew open. A man in rags and a heavy overcoat lurched toward her. A knife glinted in one hand, the blade flashing when it caught the glow from the diner.

"Hands up!" The man's rotten teeth barely showed behind his thick brown beard.

Terror seized Zoey, squeezing her lungs until she couldn't breathe. Her hands shot into the air.

"Wha...what do you want?"

"Your purse. Hand it over!" he rasped, taking one step closer.

Fear hammered against her ribs until she felt nausea and bile push their way up her throat. "I—I don't have one." She still clutched her portfolio in one hand, her fingers stinging in the cold air.

"Give me your fucking money!" His black eyes

gleamed in the dim light. He could have been any of the men she'd seen at the shelter earlier today, only they were sad and broken. This man was something else. Something evil lurked in his gaze and mirrored the spark of his blade inches from her face.

"I don't have any. I have nothing...I'm sorry." Her hands shook as she took a tiny step to the side, inching away from him. Her stomach, once so desperate for food, now clenched as she struggled to control her terror.

"Don't *lie* to me! Give me what you're holding!" Flecks of spittle shot from his chapped lips as he lunged for her portfolio.

"No!" She stepped back, dropping her hands to use the portfolio as a shield.

The man held his blade with one hand and snatched at the black leather book with the other. With a cry of panic, Zoey lost her grip and the portfolio fell to the ground. Pages and photographs scattered across the snow.

"You stupid bitch!" The man snarled and dived at her.

Zoey tried to shut her eyes, but instinct kept her lids wide open. Everything slowed down. The knife slipped between her ribs inch by painful inch. He pulled the blade back out, the cold metal sharp against her flesh as he thrust it in again. Her strangled scream was drowned out by a passing bus.

Her soul seemed to coil up tight before shooting out like a firecracker, leaving her body behind. All the work, the pain, the loss of the last two years was over. Every second she'd cried, every second she'd picked herself back up, none of it mattered anymore. Her attacker pulled the blade back out and cursed before he fled into the street.

Zoey crumpled to the ground, one hand over her side. All around her the pieces of her life, the bits she'd held on to were soaking into the soil along with her blood. Hot liquid oozed through her fingers, warming them. Pain lanced through her chest with every breath. The world spun as she slid onto her back. The night sky above was lit with a smattering of faint stars, like a handful of diamonds strewn over black velvet. Her eyes burned with tears. Blood continued to pump between her loosening fingertips as she grew too weak to keep any pressure on her wounds. A tear welled up, thick and heavy, and eased down the side of her face. The trail of moisture chilled beneath the passing breeze.

Ice dug into her shoulder blades, cold and unforgiving. Invisible rocks dropped onto her chest, and a rattling noise escaped her as she fought to breathe. Her toes were numb and her arms too heavy to move.

Muted laughter from people passing on the street seemed so far away. Would they see her? Did they hear her scream? Would they save her? The chill stealing over her warned her it was too late.

Too late for everything she'd never had a chance to do. A life unlived, a heart unloved, a soul alone.

Suddenly, the world around her darkened as a shape blotted out the winking stars. Glowing eyes, the color a wintery green, met her own. They pulled at her with the power of a sorcerer's spell. The sound of her favorite winter song, the "Carol of the Bells", began to echo in the air around them.

"Damn." His voice was rich and dark, a luscious baritone that made even her dying body tingle with lethargic awareness. He held one of her sketches, the white paper looked so sharp against the black sky. His eyes moved from her to the paper, some strange emotion she couldn't read flashing in his gaze.

The man looking down at her had the face of an angel, all angles and lines. His strong jaw, proud nose and bewitching eyes were framed with a halo of black hair from his head as he bent over more to look at her. The epitome of beauty. So handsome that she shivered. She truly was dying, and an angel had come for her soul.

He knelt down next to her. "I can save you. I only need you to trust me. Can you trust me?"

She tried to speak, and although her lips moved, no sound came out. Finally, she managed a jerky nod. Something deep inside her responded to his eyes. They emanated with warmth and the promise of safety shone from their depths. She trusted him.

Her angel did something unexpected. He raised his wrist to his mouth, bit into it and then put it against her mouth. She tasted blood and jerked away from his bleeding skin. A heavy scowl pulled his dark brows down.

"Poor sweetheart, just drink." The Irish lilt to his voice made her feel warm, despite the pain and the chill that threatened to consume her. Something about him, being so close...everything inside her seemed to stir to life in a way she hadn't realized she could.

A hand cupped the back of her head and held her captive while his wrist pressed deeper between her parted lips. Zoey gasped as the blood poured into her mouth and she was forced to swallow. The hand behind her head lightly massaged her scalp, the sensation wonderful and soothing. She relaxed into his gentle touch.

The tang of blood still coated the insides of her mouth when he pulled his wrist away.

"Easy, love, easy. You'll be okay now. I won't let any harm come to you." He cupped her face with his hands, his eyes fixed on hers, capturing her attention. "You will have no memory of tasting my blood. Only that you are safe, you are protected."

"Safe," she whispered. She had no memory to explain the oddly metallic taste in her mouth.

The man stroked her cheeks and nodded to himself before speaking again. "Would you let me take you home and care for you?" His earnest expression was so sharp that Zoey believed it. He wanted to help her.

"Y—yes." It was the only word she got out before she lost control of her body. Her lashes started to fan up and down and then fresh pain hit her like a freight train. She was barely aware of the man picking her up in his arms.

The sky above whirled, and the lights from the stars formed silver circles, like a cosmic Spirograph. She clamped her eyes shut as the man who held her leapt forward. The wind rushed around them, and her long hair whipped around her face but Zoey was lost in the aches surging through her body in tidal waves.

A second, an hour, a month, she wasn't sure when they stopped until she felt them grind to a halt. The pain faded, leaving her sore and bruised. She surrendered to exhaustion, hearing the man speak one last time as she let go.

"I want to keep you, little one. Keep you and never let you go."

Ian Kennedy stared down at the little woman in his arms as he reached his home. She was so light and he knew she should weigh more than she did. A wee waif of a body in ragged clothes. Pity stirred in his chest like a feeble bird with injured wings.

The night was quiet in the small neighborhood where he lived. No one was watching as he slipped the key into the lock of his home and entered. A gray tabby cat lounged on the couch, watching him with silver eyes.

"Lizzy," he greeted softly. The cat let out a soft purr, her tail twitching. She was one of three strays he'd rescued in recent years, much to the frustration of his friend Connor O'Shea.

Carrying the unconscious woman into his bedroom, he eased her down onto the comforter and placed a pillow beneath her head. He grit his teeth when he leaned too close to her and the irresistible scent of blood filled his senses.

But there was more than that. Even dirty and unwashed, the scent of living on the streets didn't repel his senses as they usually did when he crossed paths with the homeless while he searched for hosts to feed from at night. A tingling ache filled his mouth, and with a low curse, he tried to stop the inevitable from happening. But he failed. Twin canine teeth extended down, ready to sink into the flesh of his prey. The flesh of the woman he'd just rescued.

Ian took a reluctant step back. Space, he needed some space or else he might give into his temptation to feed on her. She'd be out for a few hours still. He'd used his innate ability to affect her body's responses to him and gently put her to sleep. It was one of the few benefits of being a vampire.

Vampire. The word still made him cringe, but there was no point in denying what he was. He'd been alive for a hundred and ninety-five years and the older he got, the stronger his abilities seemed to become. Not only could he sway the will of most humans, he also possessed a potent ability to draw his prey to him.

This seemed to be common to all his kind. The glamour, as he liked to call it, was something every vampire possessed to some degree. Something like a pheromone, it drew human prey to them, made their victims susceptible to suggestion, to desire. And with him, it created a false sense of adoration in women. Ian rarely left the house until much later in the night to avoid being around crowds. The glamour often resulted in chaos and strange behavior.

The hollow pit in his stomach reminded him he'd been on the hunt when he'd encountered the young woman being attacked. Feeding was a priority if he was to be around her without succumbing to temptation.

It was obvious she was malnourished and needed care. And more than anything, he wanted to care for her. Too many years had passed since he'd looked upon mortals as something other than…

Shutting his eyes a brief moment, he saw flashing dark eyes, heard a woman's laugh. He'd known great love for a mortal once. Lara. His body had never felt so… human since he'd been turned. But when she'd been taken from him, he'd lost that sense of life and turned back into the predator he was.

Which is why it was so puzzling that in only an instant of seeing that woman attacked tonight, he'd needed to protect her. It was as though in her moments of terror and her dying breaths, she'd called to him— much as Lara had when he'd first met her.

With a regretful sigh at leaving the woman alone,

Ian headed back outside, taking only one normal step before his body leapt into motion. The high speed of his travel, yet another one of his abilities, moved almost too fast for human sight to track. Within a minute he was in an alleyway across town, outside the diner where the woman had been wounded. The alley was empty but littered with papers. The papers from a leather portfolio lay inches from a pool of blood.

Ian knelt and began to gather the papers. Each was either a sketch or a photograph, each was captivating. He stood as he collected the binder and the last sketch. It was one of an old man, his face wrinkled, his hands gnarled as old oak tree roots clutching at a blanket as he sat on a park bench. Sadness, regret, loss of memory, all of these were locked deep into the old man's eyes. Whoever had drawn this had captured that, emotions Ian had felt every day since he'd been turned into a monster.

Something inside his chest stung and he gasped. That was odd. He'd never needed to breath before, still didn't, but his body had reacted as though it had. And the little prick of pain in his chest felt familiar, but he couldn't be sure what it was. He thumbed through the other sketches and photographs before he tucked them safely into the black binder.

"We never intervene except to feed," Connor's voice

from years ago came back to him. *"The mortals must live out their lives and we cannot intercede."*

But Ian had done just that. Saved the woman from certain death. Why? He'd been moved before in the many years he'd existed like this, but there was something about her, the way she'd protected these pieces of paper as though they were her very life. The way she saw things, the details she evoked, had been a shock to his system. Jerking him out of the seemingly endless night and forcing him beneath a sun, one that didn't burn. There was only warmth here, a craving for something he lost over a hundred years ago.

A woman that made him feel like that? After so long? That was a woman he had to save, even if only to understand why she affected him like this.

"Connor will bloody kill me when he finds out," Ian muttered to himself. He glanced around. A skinny blonde-haired waitress suddenly exited the diner's backdoor in the alley to throw a large black trash bag into the dumpster. She stilled when she saw him, her eyes first widening, then slowly turning almost slumberous.

The damnable glamour was already at work. He might as well feed while the opportunity presented itself.

"Hello," she said, wiping her hands on her apron and taking a few steps toward him.

Ian tucked the portfolio into his coat and zipped it up to keep the book in place before he started toward the woman.

"Hey there, lassie," he chuckled, hiding the hint of his fangs as they slid out. A wee bite was all he needed.

The river ran black, like water over obsidian, rushing away endlessly. Connor O'Shea leaned against the bridge railing watching the water. His fingertips clung to the stone, digging in hard enough that it would have ripped his skin apart if he'd been mortal. But he wasn't mortal, hadn't been for almost two centuries. Hunger beat at his insides, hunger for blood. It never ended, the urge to track and feed, to prey on humans, a constant reminder of what he no longer was.

Inside the pocket of his coat, his cell phone buzzed. He let out a low growl. It was probably Ian. The man never seemed to know when to leave him alone. Once, long ago, they'd been inseparable, as close as brothers. But they hadn't been that way for many years. Something was missing. He knew it. Ever since they'd lost their beloved Lara more than eighty years ago, he'd felt his body, his cursed soul, reverting to its monster state. He was on that slippery slope toward darker urges and he dreaded to contemplate what would happen to him, or worse what he'd do, once he stopped caring about life entirely. The words of Nietzsche regarding staring into the abyss came to mind.

If only I could jump, let the water consume me and swallow me in its depths.

But it wouldn't end things; he'd only wash up on shore somewhere and be that much hungrier.

He shook his head, trying to rid himself of the dark thoughts. In the distance, the city lights twinkled, heightened by a hint of merriness he sensed even from the many miles he was from home. Christmas time. A season he used to love. Now it filled him only with regret, with sorrow and longing...so much longing for a life he'd been robbed of. Being immortal was a curse. Time was frozen, like an old broken clock on a mantelpiece. The tiny metal arms never moved, never let time pass another second forward, and always reminded you that you did not work as you should. You did not belong.

I only want to move forward. So simple a wish, yet he

knew it would not be a Christmas wish he'd ever be granted.

Santa doesn't visit vampires. He chuckled, but it was a far from merry sound. *If I saw Santa Claus, I'd likely take a bite out of the jolly old man.*

His phone vibrated again and he pulled it out. Voicemail. He hated cell phones. The damn things were such a nuisance. All the chiming, the alerts, the notifications. He hit play and put it to his ear. The message was from Ian, garbled and cut out, but the main part of the message was clear. Ian had brought home a woman for Connor to feed on, but for some reason, Ian said the woman liked to be frightened as part of the excitement. Role-play. Bah. It didn't sit well with Connor, but if the woman needed it to enjoy being fed on, well, he'd oblige her.

He stepped away from the bridge and turned his attention toward the city. Time to feed.

Want to know what happens next? Buy it now at your favorite ebook or print book store. Or enjoy listening to it in the audiobook box set *Vampires and Vixens*!

About the Author

Lauren Smith is an Oklahoma attorney by day, author by night who pens adventurous and edgy romance stories by the light of her smart phone flashlight app. She knew she was destined to be a romance writer when she attempted to re-write the entire *Titanic* movie just to save Jack from drowning. Connecting with readers by writing emotionally moving, realistic and sexy romances no matter what time period is her passion. She's won multiple awards in several romance subgenres including:

New England Reader's Choice Awards, Greater Detroit BookSeller's Best Awards, and a Semi-Finalist award for the Mary Wollstonecraft Shelley Award.

To Connect with Lauren, visit her at:
www.laurensmithbooks.com
lauren@laurensmithbooks.com
Facebook Fan Group - Lauren Smith's League
Lauren Smith's Newsletter

Never miss a new release! Follow me in one or more of the ways below!

facebook.com/LaurenDianaSmith
x.com/LSmithAuthor
instagram.com/Laurensmithbooks
bookbub.com/authors/lauren-smith
amazon.com/Lauren-Smith/e/B009L54K-TC/ref=sr_tc_2_0?qid=1384012235&sr=1-2-ent